Caitlin leaned
arms around hi
for us to have as <s>much time together as possible.</s>
And if the girls at KKD can't understand that,
I'm better off not belonging to a sorority."

Julian brushed his hand against her cheek.
"Oh, Caitlin, I do love you."

She looked into his warm, gray eyes. "And I
love you, Julian."

Julian brushed her lips with his. She slid her
arms more tightly around his neck, and Julian
kissed her more forcefully. When they finally
parted, he whispered into her ear, "Caitlin, my
beautiful Caitlin, promise me you'll be mine
forever."

"Oh, Julian," Caitlin murmured, "I'll love you
always. Forever."

She rested her head against his chest, and
closed her eyes. As Julian stroked her hair, he
looked out across the room and smiled in
satisfaction. . . .

A NEW PROMISE

Bantam Books in the Caitlin Series
Ask your bookseller for the books you have missed

THE LOVE TRILOGY
  Loving
  Love Lost
  True Love

THE PROMISE TRILOGY
  Tender Promises
  Promises Broken
  A New Promise

Caitlin

A NEW PROMISE

Created by
Francine Pascal

Written by
Diana Gregory

BANTAM BOOKS
TORONTO • NEW YORK • LONDON • SYDNEY • AUCKLAND

RL 6, IL age 12 and up

A NEW PROMISE
A Bantam Book / January 1988

Conceived by Francine Pascal.

Produced by Cloverdale Press, Inc.

ISBN 0-553-26194-0

Published simultaneously in the United States and Canada

Printed and bound in Great Britain by
Hazell Watson & Viney Limited
Member of BPCC plc
Aylesbury Bucks

A NEW
PROMISE

1
___

"I really love your idea for the KKD-Omega Psi skit in the Spring Frolic," Louise Bates said to Caitlin Ryan, her voice filled with excitement. The two roommates were hurrying across the Carleton Hill University campus. "But right now it doesn't seem like spring. It seems like winter still." She huddled deeper into the turned-up collar of her coat as a sharp wind whipped a strand of long blond hair across her face.

"I know," Caitlin agreed. The cold reddened her cheeks so that they almost matched the bright red of the hat that hid much of her beautiful black hair. "But you know what they say about March; it comes in like a lion and goes out like a lamb. And we've only got about three weeks of rehearsals ahead of us. By then, there'll be leaves budding on trees, and the early flowers will be blooming." She gave Louise an encouraging smile. "Don't worry, you'll see."

"I just hope you're right." Louise shivered as

1

she quickened her steps in order to keep up with Caitlin's long strides.

"Well, don't hold me to it," Caitlin replied with a light laugh. "I'm trying to convince myself as much as I am you."

She stopped talking and burrowed her own head down into her coat to shield herself from the cold.

Caitlin and Louise were heading toward the college theater, where the first day of rehearsal for the annual variety show was being held. The show was a tradition at Carleton Hill, the small private university Caitlin had entered the previous fall as a freshman. The production was put on each year through the combined efforts of the sororities and fraternities, and the proceeds always went to charity. A different one was chosen each year, and that year the money would go to the Disabled Children's Foundation, a charity to help physically handicapped children and one close to Caitlin's heart.

"Just where did you get the idea to have the guys do a takeoff on *Swan Lake*?" Louise asked as they followed the brick path as it turned. They entered the relative warmth between two dark-red brick buildings. "I swear, it's going to be an absolute riot. Especially since most of the guys are on the football team." She giggled. "Can you imagine Stan Henderson, with his tough-guy image, in a tutu?"

"I just hope they're going to go along with it," Caitlin replied. "Actually I did something like it for a high-school fund-raiser. The guys were in a male beauty contest, and the audience loved it. Even the boys ended up having fun with it."

"Well, then why worry about our boys not wanting to do it?"

"I guess you're right. They're pretty good sports."

But a short time later, Caitlin was not so sure. She was standing in the center of the bare stage, trying to convince twelve doubtful college men to put on the wraparound practice skirts she'd borrowed from the dance department. "Come on, Darrell," she said, trying to reason with the tall, blond junior who was glaring down at her. "This is for charity."

"I'll give them money," Darrell argued, "but I'm not going to put on a skirt. Look, when I agreed to do this, I thought I was going to have to put on tights and leap around the stage like that Baryshnikov guy. That was bad enough, but these skirts? Forget it."

"But don't you see, Darrell. It's not so different from what Baryshnikov does. It's just that you'll be doing it in a tutu."

"Forget it! I'm not going to go up on a stage and have people laughing at me."

"Yeah, he gets enough of that at football practice," Josh Weston, a redheaded sophomore

3

known for his sense of humor, said. He slapped Darrell playfully on the shoulder. "Come on, Darrell, be a sport. As Caitlin says, it's all for a good cause. Look at me." With that, Josh stood on tiptoes and twirled. He nearly lost his balance before he stopped. Grinning, he added, "Pretty good, huh?"

Darrell scowled. "Okay, give me that dumb skirt." He took the skirt from Caitlin and stomped away to put it on. The other guys followed Darrell's example, and soon they were all struggling to tie the wraparound skirts over their pants.

"Thanks, Josh," Caitlin said. "You're a lifesaver. Or maybe I should say an act saver."

"It was nothing," Josh assured her. "I'm willing to bet you that Darrell ends up being the star of the show. You just have to know how to handle him, that's all. Maybe you should bring in a few cheerleaders—that would really make him happy."

"You know, Josh, you might have an idea there," Caitlin said, already working the girls into a routine in her mind.

Josh smiled. "I was kidding, Caitlin."

"Maybe, but I'm not. I'm going to give you full credit if what I'm thinking turns out to be as good as I hope it will." She could just imagine the fraternity guys in their pink costumes and wigs doing the ballet steps she had choreographed, while at the sides of the stage a group of cheerleaders cheered them on. It could be very funny, she thought, nodding to herself. Then Caitlin turned and smiled at Josh. "But right now I think we'd better get this rehearsal started. Another act has the stage in an hour."

Josh nodded. "You want me to get the guys lined up?"

"Yes. The way I showed you before," she said, looking over to make sure that Louise had the cassette player ready. "Oh, and, Josh, I guess you might as well have Darrell be the lead dancer."

"Sure thing." Josh gave her a little salute, turned around, and jogged over to where the members of Omegi Psi were waiting, dressed in their skirts.

Twenty minutes later Caitlin and Louise were standing in the wings, looks of frustration on their faces. The boys had already run through the brief routine several times.

"Are they ever hopeless!" Louise shook her head and laughed dryly. "That has got to be the tenth time in the last five minutes that Yancy has tripped."

"I know. They don't look very good, do they," Caitlin agreed. "But we have to remember that this is only the first day of rehearsals." She turned and studied the activity on the stage. "And, actually, some of the guys are really trying. Look at Darrell—he keeps improving every time. I'm sure that if he can carry a football down a field with monsters trying to knock him down, there is no reason he can't learn to do a *tour jeté*."

"You're absolutely right, Caitlin," a voice from behind them said.

Caitlin turned around. "Oh, hi, Carol," she said to the pretty junior who was her sorority big sister. "I appreciate the encouragement."

"Anytime," Carol Eaton said with a smile. She put her hand on Caitlin's shoulder. "Listen, I just wanted to remind you, and Louise, too, about the meeting at the house this evening. It's at seven, and I didn't want you to forget it."

"I did forget!" Caitlin exclaimed, covering her mouth with her hand. "I'm really sorry, Carol, but I'm not going to be able to make the meeting. I've got an appointment."

"Oh?" Carol's eyebrows lifted a fraction. "Really?" she said, not wanting to be rude and ask what the appointment was.

"Yes. It's very important. I have to go right after I'm finished here." Well, at least it was important to her. She had promised her boyfriend, Julian Stokes, she'd meet him at the Hearthside, a popular college hangout, for a hamburger. He had to work early that evening at the lab, and that was the only time she'd have to see him.

"Caitlin, this will be the second meeting you've missed in the last two weeks. And you know how important it is for pledges to attend them."

"I know," Caitlin said. "And I really do apologize. I wouldn't miss it if my appointment weren't important. But I promise I won't miss any more."

"Well, I have to tell you I'm disappointed. As your sorority big sister I'm supposed to make sure that you attend all sorority functions"—her tone softened a little—"even the boring ones, like meetings."

"I'll make the next one, honest," Caitlin promised.

"Well, okay." Carol sighed, then turned to Louise. "You're going to be there, aren't you?"

"Of course! I haven't missed one yet."

"Great!" With a pat on Caitlin's arm, Carol left.

"Caitlin," Louise said in a low voice, "you're really pushing your luck, you know. Pledges just can't miss a lot of meetings. We have to show how involved we are."

She had wanted to tell Carol that Caitlin's "appointment" was only a date with Julian, but she would have to let Carol know later in a more subtle way. But Louise was glad that Caitlin had earned Carol's disapproval at least. Maybe now she would begin to realize that dear little Caitlin Ryan wasn't so perfect as she seemed.

Caitlin defended herself, saying, "I'm working on the Frolic, aren't I? I'm really sorry if the house can't handle the fact that I want to spend some time not doing sorority things. I mean, it's not as if Julian has a lot of free time. Since he's a scholarship student, he has to keep up a high average—and in premed! And he works part-time, too. That's an incredibly demanding schedule, and when he does have a few free hours, I intend to share them with him."

"Hey!" Louise threw up her hands in protest. "I know all that. You seem to forget that I'm the one who introduced you two." She made a wry face. "I do wonder sometimes, though, if you wouldn't be better off still going with Jed Michaels. He may be a couple of thousand miles away, but at least with him you never had to drop everything whenever *he* had a few minutes free."

"I broke up with Jed for a very good reason. And I love Julian."

"Okay. All right," Louise said, stepping backward. "Don't get so mad. Forget I even brought the subject up."

"Oh, Louise, I'm sorry. I shouldn't have overreacted that way. It's just that, well, a lot of people have been telling me that I'm spending too much time with Julian, and not enough with them."

"Well, don't let them get to you," Louise advised. "They'll come around eventually." With a reassuring smile, Louise turned back toward the tape player. But as she rewound the tape for one last run-through, she thought about her roommate. The more time Caitlin spent with Julian, Louise realized, the less time she'd have to spend doing the things that had made her one of the most popular girls at Carleton Hill. And that suited Louise just fine because far from being the best friend she pretended to be, she actually disliked Caitlin. She envied Caitlin's popularity and only pretended to be her friend as a means to her own selfish ends. Louise had helped Julian split up Caitlin and Jed in the winter, and now Louise was watching what Julian would do next.

Louise turned her head slightly to look at Caitlin's beautiful profile. *If only you knew*, she said silently. *If only you knew the real Julian, you'd be singing a different tune!*

Julian Stokes arrived in front of the college theater a few minutes before Caitlin was due to meet him. It was early evening, and the temperature, which had not been all that high earlier, was dropping fast. He looked up at the dark gray cloudless sky. At least the wind had died down, he thought. Now if Caitlin only would be on time and not keep him waiting.

He turned up the collar of his coat, then glanced at his watch before thrusting his bare hands back into his pockets. It was almost five-thirty.

Julian had been dating Caitlin for almost two months, since the middle of January. But he had been laying his plan to win her since the previous fall. With determination, he had made sure every detail of his plan was in place. Soon it would all come together, and revenge would be his—revenge against Caitlin. For he did not love her. No, Julian hated Caitlin Ryan; he had since he was ten and she was seven.

His hatred had started because Caitlin's grandmother, Regina Ryan, who had raised Caitlin, owned the coal mine where Julian's father worked. Each Christmas Mrs. Ryan would come to the small town, Rock Ridge, where the Stokes family lived to hand out presents to the children. A scowl crossed Julian's handsome features as he thought about Mrs. Ryan's "generosity." One Christmas, the year he was ten, Caitlin had come to help her grand-mother. Julian had been so transfixed by the beautiful little girl in the fur-trimmed coat that he had reached out to touch her. He wasn't going to hurt her. He had only wanted to touch her, but she had cried out in horror. She had been disgusted by his worn-out clothes and ragged appearance. Julian had never forgotten that moment, and he had vowed right then that somehow, he'd get even.

Then the summer before her freshman year at Carleton Caitlin had returned to Rock Ridge. She and her friends had started a play school program for the miners' children. Julian's little sister, Kathy, had been in the group, but Julian had purposely avoided ever meeting Caitlin. But hearing about her again had refueled his need to get revenge—not only for himself but also for his father, who was dying of black lung disease after years of working in the Ryan mines. At the end of the play school when Caitlin had had the nerve to try to give little Kathy a pathetic, used doll, Julian's anger had flashed white-hot. Her boyfriend at the time, Jed Michaels, had brought the doll up to their cabin, and Julian exploded when he saw it. He smashed the doll. A fight ensued, and when it was over, Julian's plan for revenge had changed—now it included Jed.

Fate had dealt him an ace by sending Caitlin to Carleton Hill, practically delivering her into his hands. It was then that he had formed his plan for the ultimate revenge, a plan that would crush both Jed and Caitlin.

Julian had put his plan into action as soon as the fall term began. And he found a willing accomplice in Caitlin's jealous roommate, Louise. Together they had broken Jed and Caitlin up using rumors that Jed was dating his old girlfriend, Eve. And since Jed was at college in Montana, he couldn't defend himself against the lies. Meanwhile, Julian had gained Caitlin's confidence, pretending to be a sympathetic friend. At Christmas when the final breakup came, Caitlin fled to Florida with a student group to forget about her troubles. Julian made sure he was there to comfort her.

That had been two months before. In the weeks after they had returned to Carleton Hill, Caitlin and Julian's friendship had grown into what she thought was love. He smiled at how easy it had been. Caitlin had been so vulnerable that she'd fallen into his trap with very little coaxing.

But getting Caitlin to fall in love with him was only part of Julian's plan. He intended to convince her to live with him over the summer. Then she'd give herself to him completely, willingly. And when he had made her totally his, he would crush her. He could imagine the look of horror that would cross her face when he told her who he really was—that her love had not been reciprocated and that everything she felt was just a cruel joke. It would far surpass the horror she had shown on that Christmas day so long ago.

And Julian was already beginning to control her. Little by little he was separating her from her friends. Soon, he hoped, she would be turning to him for advice on everything—from what books she should be reading to the music she should be listening to, even the movies she should see. Before the semester was over, all of her thoughts would be simply mirrors of his own.

Oh, yes! Revenge is going to be sweet, so wonderfully sweet. He smiled.

"Is that smile for me?"

Julian nearly jumped at the sound of Caitlin's voice.

"Sorry I'm late," she apologized. "I got so wrapped up in some last-minute details that I didn't realize how late it had gotten."

"That's all right," he told her, smiling gently down at her as he spoke. "I never mind waiting for you." Taking his hand from his pocket, he touched her face, running one finger lightly down her cheek. He was always amazed at the clear color of her skin, like a delicate piece of porcelain. A wisp of hair had blown into her face. Tenderly, he brushed it away.

"Hungry?" he asked.

"I'm starved!" She tucked her hand into the crook of his arm. "Are we going to the Hearth-side?"

"Your wish is my command," he said. Covering her hand with his, he started toward the popular restaurant.

She walked with him, happiness glowing radiantly in her deep blue eyes.

2

"This weather is just too beautiful to be true," Louise said, stretching luxuriously. She and Caitlin were sitting on the back steps of the theater near the stage entrance. She put her long, jean-clad legs out in front of her and turned her face up to the sun. "Three weeks ago, when you said that spring would be here soon, I didn't believe you."

"Mmm," Caitlin said, her eyes closed. The sun was making her drowsy. "I didn't think it would ever get here either."

"I know it's only sixty degrees, but it feels like eighty after all that cold weather." Louise paused. "On days like today I start thinking seriously about transferring to the University of Florida. It's this nice down there pretty much year 'round."

Caitlin knew Louise was kidding and went along with the joke. "With Julian going off to medical school in the fall, I just may come with you."

"Can't you just picture us taking Surfing One-oh-one? Majoring in waterskiing?"

"Sounds fabulous," Caitlin agreed. "But I guess I'd end up missing dear old Carleton Hill."

"Me, too," Louise admitted.

They were quiet for several minutes. Then Louise spoke up again. "You know, I really think the ballet number is pretty good now. Especially since you added the cheerleader routine. I'll bet it's a real hit tonight."

"I think it's turned out well, too," Caitlin agreed. "You know, I'm really glad I worked on the Frolic, but I'm relieved that it's almost over." She sighed. "Putting on this show has been exhausting."

"Yeah, I know what you mean. But that's show biz for you," Louise added in a light tone.

Caitlin glanced at her watch impatiently. "I wish that other skit would hurry up and leave so we can have the stage. I still have—"

Caitlin stopped in midsentence as the heavy fire door above them swung open. Darrell, complete with blond wig, stuck his head out and looked both ways to make sure that no one else was around. Then he stepped outside. "Hey, you two, the stage is finally clear. Let's hurry up and get this dress rehearsal over with. I told

Anne I'd meet her in an hour, and I don't want to be late."

"Okay. We'll be right there," Caitlin said, pausing to stretch just one more time. Then she pulled herself slowly to her feet. "I think I'm going to go back to the dorm after this and take a nap," she said more to herself than to Louise. It was only after she'd gone up the stairs and into the theater that she remembered she had a date that afternoon as well. She was meeting Julian at the union. He had the afternoon free and wanted to take her to see the foreign film that was playing in the small student union movie theater. The movie was supposed to be wonderful—beautifully photographed and very moving—but just then Caitlin would have preferred a nap. But it was a chance to be with Julian, and in spite of how tired she was, Caitlin's heart beat a little faster thinking of seeing him again.

"So what did you think of the film?" Julian asked. They were sitting at a corner table in the union cafeteria. Julian's gray eyes were warm and caring. "I know it's kind of difficult to understand the subtext when you have to read the subtitles, but the central story is so forceful. I've seen it four times before, and every time I see something new."

"Really?" Caitlin had been staring a bit blankly

at the cup of coffee in front of her, and now she looked up at Julian. He was so intelligent and sensitive. Not many guys would go to see a movie so many times that dealt with a woman's love for her lost husband. But then, Julian wasn't like other boys. He was strong and sure of himself, but also kind and concerned about people.

Caitlin felt terrible that she hadn't enjoyed the movie more. She wanted so much to share with Julian the things that he enjoyed. But just then the only two things she could think of were the nap she wanted and the Frolic that night.

"Caitlin?"

All at once she realized that Julian had stopped speaking and was looking at her with great concern.

"What? I'm sorry," she apologized. "Did you ask me a question?"

"I asked if you were all right." He leaned across the table and took her hand in his. His dark brows were drawn together, and his gray eyes were troubled. "You look so tired."

"Oh, I guess I am," she admitted. "I feel like I've been juggling a thousand things at once. It's finally getting to me, I suppose." She smiled weakly. "But everything will be okay once the Frolic is over."

"I hope so," Julian said. "You've spent so much time on it recently that I've hardly had a chance to see you." He raised her hand to his lips and lightly kissed her fingertips. "I miss you when I don't get to see you every day."

"And I miss you, too, Julian." His lips brushing her fingers sent a warm thrill through her, making her feel less tired. Maybe she just needed to be with Julian more—to spend less time working so hard.

"Come on, let's get you out of here," Julian said. "I'm going to walk you back to the dorm, and I want you to promise me that you're going to get some rest." Gently letting go of her hand, he stood up and walked around the table to help Caitlin from her chair. "It was thoughtless of me to ask you to see the movie. I honestly forgot all about your dress rehearsal and how exhausted you must be."

"It's not your fault, Julian," Caitlin said as they walked to the door and started down the steps toward her dorm. "I love being with you even when I'm tired. In fact, I was just thinking—" She stopped. Would he think it was silly if she told him that just being with him gave her strength? She decided not to say it. "Oh, nothing," she finally said.

Julian gave her a questioning look but then shook his head. "I'm worried about you, Caitlin. You're doing too much. There are all those sorority meetings and the different clubs you belong to. They take up so much of your time that it's no wonder you're falling asleep on your feet."

She nodded. "I know. But I've always been involved in lots of things."

"It's not good if they make you this tired." He paused, knowing it would give his next words more power. "And not if it leaves so little time for us." He put his arm about her waist and pulled her gently to him. Then, bending his head, he kissed the top of hers. "I've been meaning to say something, but I didn't want you to take it the wrong way."

"Oh?" She leaned her head against his shoulder, breathing in his wonderful, masculine scent. "What is it?"

"Well, perhaps you should think about dropping some of your activities—just for this semester. You know, like your art club and the French club. You could rejoin them again next fall, but we'll only have till the end of this semester to be together." *It's working so perfectly*, Julian thought as he watched Caitlin consider his suggestions. "With me in med school next fall, you can join every club on campus if you want," he added.

She thought for a moment. Actually, Julian's advice made sense. And it would only be for the rest of spring term. Besides, lately she had begun to resent the activities that kept her away from Julian. In fact, she'd all but stopped going to French club, anyway. It would be better to drop out officially.

Snuggling closer to him, Caitlin sighed. "Oh, Julian, won't it be wonderful to spend all our free time together."

"Mmm-hmm." Julian stared over Caitlin's shoulder, a cold smile on his lips. *Just wonderful.*

"Oh, Caitlin!" Carol said in a shocked tone, "I think you're wrong!" It was later that same night, and Carol and Caitlin were standing backstage half an hour after the final curtain on the Spring Frolic had rung down. The show had been a terrific success and the ballet number had received the most applause—largely because of Darrell. He had been surrounded by admiring girls the moment he left the stage and was obviously loving every minute of it. A cast party was scheduled to begin as soon as everyone had changed out of his costume and the props had been put away.

"I'm sorry you feel that way, Carol," Caitlin said, hanging up the mens' skirts. "But I've already made up my mind. Besides, I'm just going to drop out of my *extra* activities. I can pick them up again next fall when Julian's gone."

"But don't you understand? You'll be giving up your friends, too. Look, I know you love Julian and you want to be with him, but not to the exclusion—"

21

"Listen, Carol!" Caitlin said, interrupting her in a firm voice. "I want to spend my time with Julian. He's more important to me than anything else right now. And I'm not giving up my friends." She shook her head. "I'm still very involved with Kappa Kappa Delta."

"Well, yes, now you are. But when is that going to change as well?"

"It's not," Caitlin reassured her. "Believe me, being a KKD is very important to me. It's just that these extra activities take up so much time."

"All right," Carol replied, giving up. "I guess there's no point in arguing with you now." She helped Caitlin slip the plastic covering over the hangers of the skirts.

"Is Julian coming to the cast party?" Carol asked a moment later.

"I invited him, but he has to work at the lab tonight."

"Oh?" Carol said. "That's too bad."

"No, it's all right." Caitlin beamed happily at her sorority sister. "I think he's going to make it up to me. He told me he has a surprise planned for me—for tomorrow. He's *so* romantic! I can't wait!"

3

"A picnic!"

"Sure, why not? It's a wonderful day for one."

It was Sunday morning, and Caitlin and Julian were standing in the lobby of Caitlin's dorm. They were both dressed in jeans, and Caitlin was wearing a bulky red sweater with a brightly patterned scarf around her neck. Julian had on a forest green, V-necked sweater. On the floor beside Julian there was a wicker picnic basket that he had borrowed from the wife of the professor who rented him his apartment. It was filled with food.

"But, Julian, this is only the end of March. Isn't it a little too cold to start thinking about picnics?"

"That's what makes the picnic special. We're going to be doing something no one else would think of doing. And can you think of a better way to spend a Sunday afternoon? I mean one

23

that a poor premed student can afford?" There was a trace of bitterness in his voice.

"Of—of course not!" Caitlin replied quickly. "It sounds wonderful."

"I'm sorry, Caitlin," Julian went on. "I didn't mean that the way it sounded. It just slipped out."

"And I'm sorry I got upset," she apologized.

He smiled to show her he understood. "You feel guilty sometimes because I don't have money and you do, don't you?" Before she could answer, he continued, "Caitlin, I've told you before that it's silly to feel that way. Money isn't important." But even as he assured her, he was glad that he had made her feel guilty for all the Ryan wealth. He wanted her to feel guilty. And the remark he had made hadn't just slipped out. He had said it on purpose. After all, it couldn't hurt to remind her that he was a poor, struggling student hoping to enter the noble medical profession while she—*and* her sorority friends—had tons of money and no such lofty ambitions.

"I know." She smiled up at him. "And you're right. Money doesn't matter." She put her hand on his arm. "Well, are we going on that picnic, or had you planned to eat all that food right here in the lobby?" She glanced around. "I admit it's quite private here since everyone seems to be sleeping in."

"I was thinking of someplace a bit more romantic," he said, his gray eyes full of promise.

"Oh? And where might that be?"

"Oh, a little place I discovered once last summer. But it's too far to walk." He paused, then wryly added, "We're going to have to take your car to get there."

"Fair enough." She nodded. "You've supplied the lunch, I'll supply the transportation."

As they walked toward the parking lot where Caitlin kept her red 280ZX, Julian mentioned missing the cast party. "I'm sorry again for not being able to make the party last night. I didn't even get a chance to see the production, and I know how hard you worked on it." He took her hand and squeezed it lovingly. "But I honestly couldn't help having to work in the lab last night. I'm afraid it's just a small preview of what my life is going to be like as a doctor—selfishly wrapped up in some medical problem."

"But, Julian, you can't call that kind of thing *selfish*." She glanced sideways at his strong profile. He was so wonderful. He had so much compassion for people. Caitlin knew he was going to make a marvelous doctor. His patients would always come first with him, and she loved him even more for that. "You were doing important work. A lot more important than our silly Spring Frolic."

"Well, maybe a little more important," Julian admitted. "Anyway, here we are," he said as they reached the car.

As they stopped beside it, Julian put down the hamper and slid his arm lightly around Caitlin's waist and pulled her to him. "You know, I haven't kissed you since yesterday afternoon. Do you suppose I might have just a small one now?"

"Mm-hmm." Caitlin let out a soft sigh. She felt so deliciously warm with Julian's arm around her. In answer, she slid her arms up about his neck and tipped her head to look up at him. But just before their lips met, Caitlin caught sight of a familiar figure several feet away. She stiffened.

For just a second she had a feeling of déjà vu. It was Matt Jenks, Jed's best friend and high school roommate from Highgate Academy, where Jed and Caitlin had met. Matt was a premed student at Carleton Hill, and she knew that he kept in touch with Jed. When she saw him, Matt was getting into his car.

"What is it?" Julian asked, confused.

"Oh—nothing," Caitlin protested. Still, she couldn't possibly kiss Julian in front of Matt. "I guess this is just too public a place after all," she said. "Let's just wait until we get to wherever we're going."

"All right," Julian said slowly. He looked at her with a small frown.

She pretended not to see it, busying herself instead by digging into the leather purse she had slung over her shoulder. Her fingers had suddenly become shaky, but finally she found the keys. She couldn't make herself look up until after she had heard Matt drive past them. For some reason, Caitlin just couldn't find the courage to meet Matt's gaze.

Julian told her to drive east, away from Carleton Hill. They traveled along back roads, marveling at how spring was beginning to turn everything green. There were gently rolling hills with picturesque farmhouses and barns. Bright bushes of yellow forsythia dotted the landscape with color.

Finally they arrived at the place Julian had wanted to show her. It was a secluded beach beside a wide, sparkling river. The beach was hidden from the road by a grove of evergreens, and some not yet flowering dogwoods. An almost nonexistent path led to a small, sunny spot beside the river.

"Oh, this is incredible!" Caitlin exclaimed as they entered the clearing. She looked around. "I wonder what it's like in the summer."

"Nicer. You can even swim." Then he looked at her. "I take that back. It's nicer now, because we're the only ones here."

"Yes," Caitlin agreed softly. Her long, dark

hair was shining in the sun, and her blue eyes sparkled with happiness.

"You're so beautiful," Julian said in a quiet voice. Without another word, he pulled her to him. She melted into his arms as he held her close and leaned his head down toward hers. Julian slid his hand up her back and gently pulled her closer as he kissed her. Caitlin felt a series of small shocks wash over her. Finally they parted.

"Hungry?" he asked her in a low, teasing voice.

"Not really."

"Come on then," he said, taking her hand. "Let's go explore."

For half an hour they wandered around the riverbank. They found small, wonderful bits of nature—a purple violet growing beside a flat rock, a bird's nest from the summer before with one small, speckled brown feather still in the bottom.

When they returned to their picnic basket, Caitlin spread out the blanket they had brought from the car. Then they sat down on it and ate hearty ham and cheese sandwiches on rolls, as well as hard-boiled eggs and cherry tomatoes. For dessert Julian had brought sensuously rich chocolate brownies he had gotten at the bakery near his apartment.

After they'd eaten, they sat in the sun drinking iced coffee. Julian reminded her that in a week it would be spring break. They wouldn't see each other for ten days.

"I can't tell you how much I'm going to miss you during the break," he said.

"I know. It's going to be terrible for me, too," Caitlin replied. In fact, she thought, it was going to be almost more than she could bear. She had come to depend on Julian so much. How did other people who loved each other ever stand being separated? she wondered.

"You're going home to Ryan Acres, aren't you?"

"Uh-huh," she said in a dull tone. She would have preferred to stay at school, but the dorms would be closed, so she had no choice. Going home to the magnificent Virginia estate where she lived with her grandmother wasn't exactly Caitlin's idea of fun. Mrs. Regina Ryan had never found it easy to demonstrate her love for her granddaughter, and since the previous summer when her grandmother had hired a new lawyer to oversee the legal matters at Ryan Mining, the tension between Caitlin and her grandmother had become more pronounced. Caitlin couldn't put her finger on what it was exactly, but there was something about the new lawyer, Colin Wollman, that made her dislike him immediately. He was just a little too smooth, a little too sure of himself. He was also slowly but surely wrapping Caitlin's grandmother around his little finger. And to make matters even worse, Colin's sister, Nicole Wollman, had been seeing Caitlin's father, Dr. Gordon Westlake. As far as Caitlin was concerned, Nicole was an ambitious man-chaser. She couldn't believe her father had failed to see through the woman's thin facade.

Caitlin knew the two Wollmans were up to no good, but she didn't have a shred of evidence against them—unless she counted that time she had seen Colin looking at Nicole in a way that was hardly brotherly.

Julian cleared his throat, and Caitlin abruptly turned to look up at him. "Oh, Julian, I'm sorry. I guess I was daydreaming," she apologized. After a brief pause she continued, "You said you were going somewhere over the break. Home?"

In all the months she had known him, Julian had never told her where his home was. She had asked before, but he had never told her. All she knew was that he came from somewhere near Washington, D.C. Maybe now she would find out where exactly.

"Unfortunately, I'm not," Julian said. "Of course I'd like nothing better than to go home for a visit." *Oh, what a lie*, he thought. It would be a cold day in hell before he'd ever go back to Rock Ridge—even for a visit. "I'm going to Boston."

"Boston?" Caitlin gave him a puzzled look. "Why?"

"I'm going there for an interview for a summer job. It's with a community services program that's attached to the medical facility at Harvard."

"Oh, that sounds wonderful, Julian." Caitlin paused. "But why Boston? I mean, since you're planning to go to UVA Medical School, wouldn't it be more practical to try to get a job in Charlottesville?"

"I suppose it would," Julian said. "But I've also applied for another position—one to work with a Dr. Henry Kramer at Harvard. He specializes in spinal cord injuries, and he's working on some new techniques that could revolutionize the field. Premed students from all over the country are applying for the position as well, so the chances of my getting it are slim. But if I don't get the position, this other job is a good backup, because it would still give me a chance to observe Dr. Kramer's work."

"Oh. That makes sense," Caitlin said. She wanted to be enthusiastic for Julian's sake, but all she could think of was that Boston was a long way from Virginia. "It's all still up in the air right now, isn't it?" she asked hopefully.

"Yes." Julian smiled and reached over to take her hand in his. "And I'd rather think about right now and being with you in this beautiful place."

"Oh, Julian, I feel the same way," Caitlin replied, her voice full of love. "I wish I could take this moment and wrap it up and keep it forever."

4

Jed Michaels stood beside his mailbox in the narrow, rustic Montana Agricultural College post office. He looked at his mail for the day: a brochure from a custom boot maker, a letter from his father at the ranch, and one from Virginia.

His fingers tightened on the envelope as he noted Matt Jenks's return address in the upper left-hand corner. In Matt's last letter he had said that Caitlin was dating someone new. Jed had nearly gone crazy at the news. It was true that he and Caitlin had fought at Christmas, but Jed still hoped that she was just taking a long time to get over being angry with him.

The trouble had started in the fall when Caitlin had discovered that Eve Towers, Jed's old girlfriend, was going to Montana Agricultural, too. Jed had known that Caitlin would be upset if she knew that Eve was at the same college as he, so he hadn't told her. He hadn't exactly decided not to tell her, it was really an unconscious decision. But somehow Caitlin had found out. Then Caitlin had accused him of lying to her, and even though that wasn't exactly true, Jed realized now that he should have told her about Eve from the start.

After all, Caitlin and Eve were hardly friends. During the past summer when Caitlin had been visiting Jed's ranch, Eve had gone so far as to cut the cinch on Caitlin's saddle so Caitlin would lose a race. Caitlin's quick thinking had saved her from sure disaster.

But Eve was no longer the same schemer she had been. She and Jed certainly weren't dating again, but they had become friends. The trouble was, as hard as Jed had tried to explain that to Caitlin, she just wouldn't understand. Finally Jed had gotten angry at her for not trusting him, and things had slowly deteriorated.

The end had come when he couldn't go to Virginia to be with Caitlin at Christmas as they'd planned. He had called her from the Towerses' ranch on Christmas Day, but when Caitlin had found out that he was at Eve's house, she had slammed the phone down in his ear. Of course, he realized now that it had been a mistake to admit he was calling from Eve's ranch, but he couldn't help it. There had been a storm, and the lines were down at his own place. Still, he thought, that shouldn't have been a reason to end their relationship.

Jed looked down at the letter in his hand. He'd written to Matt, asking him to see what he could find out about the guy Caitlin was dating. In one way, Jed was afraid to open it, but in another, he wanted to rip it open before another second went by. Looking around at the small, crowded room, he decided he had better wait until he was alone.

Tucking the letter, along with his other mail, into the inside pocket of his sheepskin jacket, Jed pulled the brim of his western hat firmly down over his brow and pushed through the post office door into the cold Montana air. Bowing his head and hunching his shoulders against an icy wind, he went down the steps and cut across an open field in the direction of the student union. It was late in the afternoon, and he hoped to find an empty table in the corner.

He did. He took out the letter and dropped it on the table, then put his hat and coat on an empty chair. The letter in front of him, Jed sat down, took a deep breath in order to calm himself and then slit the envelope open. The letter was on lined yellow sheets from a legal tablet.

Jed unfolded it, read the opening paragraph, then quickly skimmed down to the part about Caitlin.

I know you want to know what's going on with Caitlin, but there isn't much to tell. I rarely run into her anymore, and when I do, she ignores me. Like I told you in my last letter, I think Caitlin started dating this guy, Julian Stokes, when she came back from Christmas break. They're still going out, and from what I hear, it looks serious.

I hate to say this, Jed, but he seems to have it all together. Julian is your basic tall, dark, and handsome guy, who also happens to be a brilliant premed major. I know he's smart because he's the TA in one of my classes and because we were friendly for a bit at the beginning of the year. Frankly, I really admire his abilities.

I don't know a lot about him except that he's a real loner. He doesn't belong to a fraternity, and he doesn't seem to be involved in any other school activities. He has a part-time job at the lab (I think he's on a scholarship), so maybe he just doesn't have time.

But he does have time to date Caitlin, Jed thought, pounding his fist on the table in frustration.

He looked back at the letter again. There was no more news about Caitlin, so he skimmed the rest. With a heavy sigh, Jed refolded the pages and returned the letter to the inside pocket of his jacket.

Jed had never felt so helpless. He was almost two thousand miles from Caitlin, and just then, it seemed like two million. Spring break was only a week away, and Jed wished desperately that he could get on a plane and go to Virginia to see her. But that was impossible. And Caitlin had found someone new, anyway.

Jed looked out a nearby window at the bare branches of a row of aspens, and then he looked at the ground below. A few dirty patches of snow remained on the muddy ground. In Virginia, the trees would already have leaves on them, he thought, and the grass would be thick and lush. Jed thought back to the day he'd arrived at Highgate Academy, in Virginia.

It had been Jed's father's idea to send him East to finish up his last two years of high school at a prestigious private school. Highgate's respected academic reputation would help him get into one of the Ivy League colleges, where he hoped to study prelaw. And certainly Jed had benefited by going to Highgate. He'd been accepted at Carleton Hill, which had one of the best prelaw programs in the country, as well as by several Ivy League schools. But then his father had asked him to reconsider his career decision and think about staying in Montana to work the ranch. Jed loved both the ranch and his father, but he also knew that he had to follow his heart—and that meant a career in law. So they had reached a compromise: Jed would spend one year at agricultural college, and then he could return to the East if he wanted. It had seemed like a fair bargain at the time, but because of it, he had lost Caitlin.

Jed thought about the first time he had met Caitlin. He didn't really like her, dismissing her as a spoiled rich girl who always got what she wanted. She was also a terrible flirt, and he had always hated girls who came on too strong. But then he'd gotten to know Caitlin, and he had come to realize why she was so self-centered. It was really a protective shield that she'd put up to keep from being hurt any more than she already had been. She had grown up in a totally loveless household, which was run by her domineering grandmother, the powerful Regina Ryan.

Jed closed his eyes, and put his hand over them, resting his elbow on the table. He loved Caitlin so much—he always would. But how could he win her back? And what had he done that had been so terrible that it had driven her away from him in the first place?

"Hi, Jed."

Jed opened his eyes and looked up. A slim, pretty girl with long blond hair was looking down at him. She was wearing jeans, a heavy down jacket, and had a canvas backpack slung over her shoulder.

"Oh, hi, Eve." *Damn!* He didn't want to talk to her. He didn't really want to talk to anybody.

Maybe if he didn't invite her to sit down, she would just go away.

"Thanks, I will," she said brightly. Pulling out a chair on the opposite side of the table, she slid gracefully into it. She tossed her jacket onto the empty chair where Jed had left his, then rested her elbows on the table.

"Will what?" Jed asked, confused.

"Sit down, of course." She flashed him a brilliant smile. "You were going to ask me to, weren't you?"

"Yeah, sure," Jed said in a dry tone. What else could he say?

"Boy, are you a grouch today!" Eve observed, not bothered in the least by Jed's unenthusiastic response.

"Sorry," he apologized. "I guess my mind was somewhere else."

"In Virginia?" She looked at Jed, her turquoise eyes full of sympathy she didn't feel. "It's rough breaking up with someone, isn't it? It hurts for a long time."

Does it ever, Eve thought as she looked at Jed. It had been years since Jed had broken up with her, and she still hadn't gotten over him. But now she was going to get him back. She was going to make him love her again. But first she had to play the sympathetic, understanding friend. Then, when Jed realized how true a friend she really was, when she'd regained his complete trust, Eve would lure him back into her arms.

"Yeah, it does hurt," Jed said in an angry tone. "It's the worst kind of torture there is."

"You're not kidding," Eve agreed.

Jed looked at her, a puzzled expression on his face.

"I know what you're going through, Jed," Eve said, putting a hand on his arm. "Things haven't been going all that well in the romance department for me, either."

"I didn't know you were going with anyone, Eve," Jed said, looking up at her with interest. "What happened?"

"Buck Thomas and I started seeing each other near the end of fall term. He was so kind and gentle. I really thought we had something good." Eve let her lower lip tremble slightly. "Then, last week, he told me he didn't want to see me anymore. Just like that—over." Eve hadn't really been dumped by Buck. In fact, they'd only dated once, months before.

"I'm sorry. I guess I never noticed you two together that much. Just shows I really have been preoccupied, huh?" He shook his head.

"That's okay, Jed," Eve said. "Really, I understand." She gave his arm a reassuring squeeze. "You know, the reason I stopped to talk to you was because you looked so sad. I thought maybe an understanding listener might be just what you need." She paused to give him an encouraging smile. "Sometimes it helps to talk to someone."

"Thanks, Eve. I appreciate the offer, but not right now. I guess talking about Caitlin still hurts too much."

"Don't worry, I understand." Eve withdrew her hand. "But remember, I'm always here if you change your mind. I just want to be your friend, Jed."

"You are, Eve. And thanks for trying to help," Jed said sincerely.

"Well, I'll see you later," Eve said, standing up. She pulled on her coat, grabbed her backpack, and headed for the door. There was a satisfied smile on her face.

5

Caitlin had just gotten back to Carleton Hill, having spent spring break at Ryan Acres avoiding Nicole and Colin. She had managed to see her father alone on one occasion and was grateful for at least one visit without Nicole.

It was late afternoon, and she was unpacking the small suitcase she had brought home with her. Louise, who had already unpacked, was sitting on her bed polishing her nails. As Caitlin hung up the last two blouses in her closet, the phone rang.

"Will you get that?" Louise asked, looking over at her roommate. "My nails are wet."

"Sure," Caitlin replied. She answered the phone, and a moment later she cried out happily, "Julian, I can't believe it's really you— dinner? Not much, I guess. The dining hall won't be open until morning. I was thinking of going over to the Hearthside for a hamburger." She paused. "Do you want to meet me?"

"I was thinking about something a little more romantic, to be honest. How about if I cook you dinner at my apartment?"

"Oh, that sounds wonderful!"

"Well, I'm warning you," Julian cautioned. "I'm not the greatest cook in the world."

"Don't worry. If it's anything like the picnic you fixed, it'll be great. Besides," she added, speaking in a low voice so Louise couldn't hear, "the most important thing is seeing you again. Oh, Julian, you don't know how much I've missed you."

"Why do you think I planned this dinner?" Julian's voice was low and warm, too. "I knew there was a chance that you'd already have eaten or that you'd be too tired to come over, but—"

"That will never happen," Caitlin broke in. "I'll always want to be with you whenever I have the chance."

"I feel the same way, Caitlin. I can hardly wait to see you. How long do you think it'll take you to get ready?"

Caitlin looked down at her sweatpants and sweatshirt. "I'll be over in about an hour, okay?"

"If you can't make it sooner, I guess that'll have to do," Julian replied. "I'll start counting the minutes."

As soon as she hung up, Caitlin spun around

with joy. Then she looked over at Louise. "Did you hear? Julian is making dinner for me."

"I heard that much," Louise said wryly. "You know, Caitlin, you and Julian are together so much, you should just give up and move in together."

Caitlin ignored Louise's remark. "What am I going to wear?" she moaned, walking over to her closet and opening the door. It was bulging with clothes. Caitlin stared at the carefully arranged row of dresses, pants and tops, absentmindedly twirling a strand of hair as she considered the choices. Then she reached in and pulled out a pair of linen pants and a cranberry-colored cotton sweater. Holding them in front of her, she turned to her roommate. "What do you think, Louise?"

Louise looked up at Caitlin. "Perfect," she said in a flat voice. "If you drop spaghetti sauce on that top, it won't even show."

"Spaghetti sauce?"

"Of course." Louise inspected her newly polished nails. "What else would a guy cook for dinner?"

"I bet you thought I was going to cook spaghetti, didn't you?" Julian asked as he carried two cups of steaming coffee over to the table in front of the couch. The dinner dishes had already been cleared away.

"Well," Caitlin admitted with a grin, "Louise did warn me that you might."

Julian set the cups down and went back over to the little kitchen alcove. He poured some milk into a small pitcher and took it, along with the sugar bowl, over to the couch.

He sat down on the couch beside Caitlin. She was curled up in the corner, one foot tucked under her. She looked so lovely, he thought, with wisps of her dark hair curling softly around her perfect oval face. The low-necked cotton sweater she was wearing made him want to reach out and touch the soft skin of her throat. "Sorry I've only got instant coffee," he apologized in a low tone.

"I don't mind instant," Caitlin assured him. She smiled softly, and the look in her eyes was warm. "And I loved dinner. You make wonderful linguini with clam sauce. I thought you'd just open a jar of sauce and heat it. The clam sauce really was good. And the table was so beautiful—the candles and the flowers." Caitlin paused, listening to the romantic music playing on the classical radio station. "I love Grieg. The *Peer Gynt* Suites in particular are so beautiful. When I hear that music, I think of misty hills and castles and—"

"Lovers meeting beside a beautiful river in the moonlight," Julian finished. "I picked it out because it reminded me of the day we had our picnic."

"Yes," Caitlin answered dreamily. "That was such a lovely place. I'm glad you took me there."

"Caitlin—" Julian felt himself being drawn to her. He wanted to gather her in his arms and hold her close. The crisp, woodsy smell of her perfume made him light-headed. *Get ahold of yourself, Julian,* he warned silently. *The idea is to get Caitlin under your spell, not the other way around. Willpower, Julian, willpower.* He reached for his coffee cup.

"So what did you do over the break?" he asked. "I remember you said you were looking forward to riding your horse again. What's his name? Duster, right?"

"Uh—yes," Caitlin answered, feeling a little confused. She was sure that Julian had been about to kiss her. And she'd wanted him to. But now he was almost distant, asking her polite, impersonal questions. *What's going on?* she wondered. "I did get in some riding," Caitlin finally answered. "The ground's still pretty muddy from the winter, though."

Julian looked at Caitlin closely. He'd almost let his longing for her overrule the hatred he felt for her. Sometimes when he was close to her, he almost let himself believe that they were like any other young couple in love—that they would soon be building a life together. But that was ridiculous. He had to remember that his real reason for making her fall in love with him was to get revenge for that Christmas so many years before. He had to separate her from her friends to finish setting up his plans for that revenge.

"So how about you, Julian?" Caitlin asked, pouring milk into her coffee and stirring it. "What happened in Boston?"

"Everything went really well," Julian said. "I got the job with the community services program. And not only that, I spoke to Dr. Kramer's secretary, and—"

"Well, did you get it?" Caitlin asked impatiently.

"Hold on and I'll tell you," Julian replied, laughing. "She said that the number of applicants had been narrowed down to sixty. I'm not in, by any means, but I'm still in the running."

"That's terrific, Julian! I'm so glad." Caitlin's face suddenly became serious. "But still, sixty is a lot of applicants."

"I'm still sure I've got a good chance of getting it," he said with confidence. And he meant it. He knew he was good. All he had to do now was make sure Caitlin would agree to go to Boston with him. As Julian thought about what would happen then, the corners of his mouth turned up in a satisfied grin.

"Oh, I'm positive Dr. Kramer will choose you," Caitlin said.

"Your confidence in me means a lot, Caitlin," Julian replied smoothly. Reaching out, he covered her hand with his, letting his smile fade. "There's only one thing that makes me wish I weren't going, though."

"What's that?" Caitlin asked, her voice full of concern.

"We'll be so far away from each other when I'm in Boston. I wish we could spend every moment together until then."

"Oh, I do, too, Julian. And we can be together most of the time, except for classes, when you're in the lab, or I'm over at the KKD house, of course."

"That's just it—" Julian began, then he stopped and shook his head. "Oh, never mind. I shouldn't have said anything."

"What is it?"

"Nothing. Really," Julian answered.

"Julian, tell me. What were you going to say?"

"Well, if you insist. Caitlin, you know how crazy my hours at the lab are. I can never be sure when I'm going to be able to make time for us. And so many times recently when I've called your room, you're out—over at your sorority house or something. I know I can't blame you— KKD means a lot to you, and I'd never ask you to give it up. It's just that, well, I hate the time it takes away from us," he said, knowing his voice sounded sincere and convincing. He just hoped it would make Caitlin think of dropping out of the sorority. Holding his breath, he waited for her next words.

Caitlin thought for a moment, and then the perfect solution occurred to her. "Why don't I just unofficially drop out of KKD until after you graduate? As long as I make it to most of the meetings, they won't ask me to depledge. And that way, I'll have more time to see you."

"Oh, Caitlin, don't do that. I don't want you to jeopardize your membership." *Oh, yes, I do,* he countered silently, looking into her troubled blue eyes.

"But I won't be doing that," she said quickly. "I mean, maybe I will, but Carol's already angry at me for missing so many meetings. It won't make that big a difference. And I can make up for it in the fall after you're gone." She uncurled her feet, leaned toward him, and circled her arms around his neck. "All I want right now is for us to have as much time together as possible. And if the girls in KKD can't understand that, I'm better off not belonging to a sorority."

Julian brushed his hand against her cheek. Kissing her forehead, he said, "Oh, Caitlin, I do love you so very, very much."

She looked into his warm, gray eyes, feeling a wave of tenderness wash over her. "And I love you, Julian."

Julian brought his face closer to hers and

brushed her lips with his. Caitlin pressed herself closer to him and kissed him back. Then she slid her arms more tightly around his neck, and Julian kissed her more forcefully. When they finally parted, he whispered into her ear, "Caitlin, my beautiful Caitlin, promise me you'll be mine forever."

"Oh, Julian," Caitlin murmured, letting out a soft sigh. "I'll love you always. Forever."

She rested her head against his chest and closed her eyes. As Julian stroked her hair, he smiled in satisfaction.

6

Caitlin was breathing hard. She could feel tiny beads of sweat running down her back. Still, she didn't want to stop running. When she ran hard and long enough, she stopped thinking about anything except the next step, and the next, and the next. Since she didn't have Duster at Carleton Hill to ride every day, she had had to take up running to keep in shape. She also played tennis, but lately she found she preferred a fast run around the campus.

Finally, after three miles, Caitlin felt a cramp developing in her side. It was time to stop. Turning off the path, she bent at the waist and clasped her toes with her hands. She was gulping in breaths of air, and her heart was hammering in her chest. Soon, however, as she walked to cool down, the hammering slowed.

Caitlin sat down finally and wrapped her arms around her knees. How great it would be, she thought, to be able to just stay right where she was for the rest of the day. She would have been happy just to be by herself, with only the singing of the birds for company and the sweet smell of the grass and flowers to evoke simple pictures of spring. In a lot of ways, the area she had been running in reminded her of the back fields at Ryan Acres. She briefly remembered the ride through those fields she had taken with her grandmother the week before.

Caitlin had never known her mother. Laura Ryan, Caitlin's mother, had been Regina Ryan's only child. When Laura was in college, she had fallen in love with the man Caitlin now knew and lovingly accepted as her father, Dr. Gordon Westlake. But at the time he and her mother had been seeing each other, he was just a poor boy from the Virginia mountains—hardly a suitable match for Regina Ryan's beautiful and wealthy daughter.

When Mrs. Ryan learned of their relationship, she whisked Laura away to Europe. It was only after they had arrived that she learned that Laura was going to bear Gordon's child. Tragically, Laura died when Caitlin was born. Embittered and blaming Gordon Westlake for her daughter's death, Regina Ryan returned to America with Caitlin. She swore that he would never know he had a child.

And Regina Ryan had kept her secret for sixteen years. She raised Caitlin alone, demand-

ing perfection from the young girl, but showing
very little love. Then, when she was sixteen,
Caitlin met her father for the first time. She had
gone to Meadow Valley Hospital, where he was
the director, to try to help a sick friend. But the
meeting was far from the tender reunion it
might have been. Because her grandmother had
filled Caitlin with lies about her father—telling
her that he'd abandoned her—Caitlin hated him
at first. But finally Mrs. Ryan had told Caitlin the
truth, and now Caitlin and Dr. Westlake were
closer than most fathers and daughters.

A small movement a few feet away inter-
rupted Caitlin's thoughts. She glanced over and
saw a fat brown bird struggling to pull a worm
from the ground. She laughed lightly. "You're
too fat already, my friend. If you eat that worm,
you won't be able to fly."

As if in answer to her remark, the bird let go of
the worm, hopped a few feet, and then flew to a
low branch of a nearby tree. It sat there, watching Caitlin.

"Are you trying to tell me that you'd like me to
go away so you can have your breakfast in
peace?" She smiled. "All right." Laughing, Caitlin jumped to her feet and began jogging slowly
away. It was time for her to go back to the dorm
anyway.

As she cut across the field, she thought about
Julian and about a conversation she'd had the

night before with another pledge, Lisa Whit-
more. There was no doubt in Caitlin's mind that
Julian was more important to her than membership in a sorority. The problem was that her
friends didn't think so. Lisa had reminded her
that she was always with Julian, to the exclusion
of being with any of her other friends. "No one
even asks you to go anywhere anymore," she
said. "Haven't you noticed that you don't get
very many phone calls now? No one bothers,
because they know you'll just say you've got
plans with Julian."

Lisa and the other sorority members just
didn't understand, Caitlin thought. It was as if
none of them had ever been in love. If only she
could really sit down and talk with someone
about how to handle the problem, Caitlin
thought. If only there was someone who wasn't
involved, someone who could look at everything objectively.

Ginny Brookes, her best friend and roommate
from Highgate, would be the perfect person.
Ginny, who had more common sense than
anyone Caitlin knew, would know just what to
do. But she and Ginny were no longer speaking.
In fact, Ginny hated her now. And it was all
because of Julian. *How ironic*, Caitlin thought.
There she was, thinking that Ginny would be
the one person with whom she could discuss her

problems, but those problems involved the very person who had split Ginny and Caitlin apart.

It happened during their trip to Florida over Christmas break. They had gone with a bunch of kids from Carleton Hill to Fort Lauderdale; Julian had been in the group. Ginny, who had met Julian a couple of times and had a wild crush on him, was envisioning a romantic week in Julian's arms. But instead, while he was comforting Caitlin after her breakup with Jed, Julian had awakened romantic feelings in her. And it had been Caitlin who had ended up in Julian's arms for just one evening, leaving Ginny hurt and angry.

Caitlin felt terrible when she realized what had happened. When she'd gotten back to their room that night, Ginny pretended to be asleep. And the next morning she went to the airport while Caitlin was on the beach.

Caitlin had wanted to call her friend immediately after she received Ginny's note accusing her of stealing Julian, but Julian told her not to. He said Caitlin had done nothing wrong and it would be better to give Ginny time to realize that. If anyone else had made that suggestion, Caitlin would have ignored it. She knew that it was always best to apologize quickly even if she hadn't been in the wrong. But Julian had been so persuasive that she finally had given in to his suggestion.

That had been just a little more than three months before. The time had only deepened the distance between Caitlin and her former best friend. Caitlin missed Ginny enormously, but she didn't know how to apologize after so much time had passed. Also, she was afraid she'd hurt Ginny more by telling her that *she* was in love with Julian.

Caitlin slowed down as she got closer to the dorm. She reached up and pulled the sweatband off her forehead, shaking her head to free her hair. Pausing at the steps to the dorm, she did some leg stretches to keep from getting stiff. Then she ran lightly up the stairs, saying hello to a couple of girls coming down. She would take a quick shower, then dress. Julian was meeting her for a late breakfast at the Hearthside.

Caitlin could hardly wait to see him. She smiled to herself. It had been only hours since they had been together, but it seemed like days. Being with Julian made everything else seem unimportant by contrast.

7

"Ready for breakfast?" Julian smiled down at Caitlin as he put his arm around her shoulders and pulled her to him in a warm embrace. They had just met in front of the Hearthside.

"I went for a long run this morning, and I'm absolutely starved." Her long, dark hair was still slightly damp from the shower, and tiny tendrils curled sweetly about her face. She had dressed in white pants, and a light, but bulky, cotton sweater. The deep blue of the sweater matched her eyes. "I hope we're not too late for the breakfast special."

"I don't think so," Julian said. He glanced at his watch, turning his wrist against her shoulder so he could see the time. "No. We still have plenty of time. And, to tell the truth, I'm hungry, too." Tiny laugh lines appeared around his eyes as he smiled at her. "Good news always affects me that way."

"News?" Caitlin asked with interest. "What news?"

"Ah! You must wait until we get inside and get our breakfast. Then I'll tell you," Julian said teasingly.

"Well then, come on." Caitlin playfully pulled at his shirt. "What are we waiting for?"

Even though the restaurant was crowded, Caitlin and Julian managed to find a booth near a window. They ordered, and in a short time the waitress returned with scrambled eggs and bacon for Julian, and a mushroom and cheese omelet for Caitlin.

"All right, time's up," Caitlin said. "I'm not going to eat a single bit of this until you tell me what's going on. And an omelet isn't good cold, so you'd better hurry up."

"Threats will get you nowhere. I will only tell you because I can hardly wait another minute." That much was true. What he had to tell her was so wonderful that he didn't want to keep it to himself a minute longer.

But it was mainly wonderful because he now could finalize his revenge against Caitlin. If Caitlin would agree to go to Boston with him, he would have her exactly where he wanted her— in Boston, with him, for the summer, and they could finally sleep together!

He looked at her then, sitting there across the table from him, anxiously waiting to hear his news. He could imagine how that beautiful face would look when she realized just how she had been used, when he finally told her who he really was, why he had ruined her relationship with Jed, and why he'd made her think he loved her.

"Julian!" Caitlin cried, leaning toward him. "Come on!"

"I got a call this morning from Dr. Kramer."

"Dr. Kramer!" Her eyes were wide with surprise. "Oh, Julian, does that mean what I think it means?"

"I got the position." He couldn't help grinning. "I got it!"

"Oh, Julian, how wonderful! I'm so excited for you. But"—she paused, shaking her head in confusion—"so soon? I mean, we were just talking about it last night, and you said when you were there he had only narrowed the field down to sixty."

"I know. I guess Dr. Kramer made the final decision just after I was there because they called at eight-thirty this morning and told me I had it."

"When do you start?"

"Right after finals."

"What about graduation?"

"I'll be in Boston already, and I won't have time to come back down here for it. Besides, walking across a stage and accepting a piece of paper just doesn't mean much to me. Getting this position does."

"I understand," Caitlin said in a faraway voice. She was thinking about how distant Boston was and how she wouldn't be able to see Julian constantly during the summer.

"But here's the best part," Julian went on. "I want you to come to Boston with me."

"What?" Caitlin asked, unsure she'd heard him correctly.

"I want you to come to Boston this summer," Julian repeated. "Now that I have the position with Dr. Kramer, the job with the community services program is open. If you took that job, we could spend the entire summer together."

"Oh, Julian, I'd love to. I can't think of anything more wonderful than spending the entire summer with you. But—" she hesitated.

"But what?" Julian reached across the table and took Caitlin's hand. "Listen, I know you could do the job. You've got a good background for working with disabled children. You told me once that you helped a little boy who had been crippled when you were in high school—that would be more experience than most people could have."

"Yes, that's right, but—" A mix of painful and happy memories flooded her mind as she thought about Ian Foster. He had lost the use of his legs because of her carelessness, but then he had walked again, mainly as a result of her care.

"And what about that play school project you organized last summer?" Julian went on. Caitlin had told him about the project she and Jed and Matt Jenks and Emily Michaels had run in Rock Ridge the summer before. Of course he'd already known about it, but he couldn't tell Caitlin that.

"Yes," she said with a smile. "I loved doing that. It was really rewarding working with those kids."

"Well, then, you'd be terrific for the job in Boston. And I think you can even earn class credits at the same time."

"Well, that would definitely be a plus. Still"— her brow furrowed—"there must be a waiting list or something. You know, people who've already applied and are waiting to see if anyone drops out."

"But maybe they don't have one. Look, I can't promise anything, but maybe it would help if I called. It won't hurt to try. And even if you don't get the job there, there must be hundreds of opportunities for jobs in Boston."

"All right, suppose I do get the job. What about my grandmother? I'm not sure she'd let me go."

"But it's not just any job, Caitlin—it's at Harvard. Surely she couldn't have any objections to your working at a place as prestigious as

61

Harvard. Especially considering the fact that you might be able to earn college credits."

"Maybe," Caitlin replied doubtfully. "But where would I live? I know my grandmother would want to make sure I'd be living somewhere she considered suitable."

Here goes, Julian thought. The moment he'd been worried about had arrived. He had to say everything in just the right way or Caitlin wouldn't take that final step into his trap. Julian took a deep breath. He put everything he had into making his voice sound filled with love.

"You could stay with me," he began, holding her hand tightly. "Wait, don't say anything until I explain. See, I found out this morning that I can house-sit for a professor who is spending the summer in Europe. I understand it's a beautiful big apartment. You could just tell your grandmother that you'd be staying in a dorm. You could arrange for a dorm room, a mailbox, everything. Your grandmother would never find out you weren't actually living there. What do you think?" Julian watched Caitlin's face, but her expression made it hard to tell what she was thinking. *Would she agree?* he wondered anxiously.

"Oh, Julian!" She looked at him for a long moment. "I don't know what to say."

Damn! he thought. He'd been wrong to ask her so soon. He'd thrown too much at her at once. Julian scowled. Had he blown everything? It certainly seemed as though he had.

"Oh, Julian," Caitlin repeated. It would be all right, she thought. They'd have their own rooms, but they could be together all the time—long talks late into the night, breakfast together every morning. She looked radiant.

"Yes?"

"Julian, I can't think of anything I'd rather do than share an apartment with you this summer," she said breathlessly.

"Really?" A feeling of triumph bubbled up inside him. "You mean it?"

"Yes. Yes, really!" she replied, laughing happily.

"Caitlin," he said as he leaned across the table and kissed her. "Oh, I do love you, Caitlin." For that amount of time, he really meant it.

"And I love you, Julian," she said, her voice low and warm. "Very, very much."

8

As he had promised Caitlin he would, Julian called the director of personnel for the community service program the following day. As it turned out, the director was delighted that Julian had someone to recommend to take his position. She promised she'd forward an application to Caitlin immediately.

The application had arrived a week later, and Caitlin was asked to provide two references. She decided to ask Mrs. Van Allen, the woman from Highgate who had been the faculty sponsor at the play school project in Rock Ridge, to write one of them. After much deliberation, she decided to ask Mrs. Brand to write the other one. Mrs. Brand was the supervisor of the volunteer staff at Meadow Valley Hospital, where Caitlin had worked for part of one summer and where her father was director.

When she couldn't reach Mrs. Brand, Caitlin decided to call her father, to see if he could leave her a message. She wanted to tell him about her summer plans, anyway. Caitlin was sure that he would be thrilled to see her taking an interest in a field so closely related to his own.

Much to her surprise, he was not pleased. "Oh, Caitlin, I'm disappointed," he said when she told him her news. "I've been looking forward to having you at Ryan Acres all summer. I wanted to spend lots of time with you. But that'll hardly be possible with you in Boston."

"But, Father, even if I do get the job, it won't start until July," Caitlin protested. "I'll be at home for all of June, and we can spend lots of time together."

Dr. Westlake paused. "You really want to spend two of the hottest summer months in a city?" he asked.

"Well, the job really sounds terrific. And it's a great opportunity to work with kids again," she said. She decided not to mention Julian. Her father didn't know him, and he might suspect that she only wanted to go to Boston to be with him—which, she suddenly realized, wasn't entirely true. "Besides," she went on, "the program is affiliated with Harvard, and I might even be able to earn a couple of credits."

"College credits, huh? And Harvard's not too shabby a name to have on one's resume, either." Dr. Westlake paused, then laughed. "Well, I guess I can't fight that. All right, I'll find Mrs.

Brand and ask her to write a letter for you. I'll
tell her to make it so glowing that they couldn't
possibly refuse you."

"Not *too* glowing, please," Caitlin warned,
laughing in return. "They'll think I've paid her
off or something."

"Can I help it if I'm proud of you? Hurry
home."

"I'll be there soon. And just remember, I'll be
at Ryan Acres for the whole month of June.
You'll probably be so sick of seeing me that
you'll be glad to have me leave for Boston."

"Never!" Dr. Westlake protested. Then he
paused, and Caitlin heard him say something to
someone, probably Miss Parks, his secretary.
Moments later he was back on the line. "Sorry,
honey, I've got to run. I have to go look in on a
patient."

"All right, Father," Caitlin said. "Thank you
again. I love you."

"I love you too, honey." He hung up, and
Caitlin had sat there for a moment, just thinking
how fortunate she was that they found one
another after being separated for sixteen years.

Now it had been three weeks since she'd returned the application. Still, she hadn't heard a
thing. It was getting close to the end of the
school year as well. Exam schedules had already

been posted. Caitlin was worried. What if she didn't get the job? Then there would be no real reason to spend the summer in Boston. At least, no reason that she could tell her grandmother. Oh, she could visit Julian, but it wouldn't be the same as staying there.

Then late one afternoon, when she had just about given up hope, she looked in her mailbox to find a fat envelope. The return address on the corner was the community service program at Harvard. Ripping it open, she scanned the cover letter. A wide grin lit up her face as she hurried to the elevator and pushed the up button.

"Louise! Louise, guess what?" she called out as she burst into their room a few minutes later.

"Mmm, what?" Louise answered vaguely, not looking at Caitlin. She was sitting cross-legged on her bed, a volume of Flannery O'Connor's short stories on her lap.

Caitlin plopped down on the side of her bed. "Louise, did you just hear me?" she asked as she stared at her roommate. "Something wonderful has just happened."

"Okay, okay." Louise closed her book and turned to her roommate. She noticed the envelope Caitlin was holding. "Did you win one of those Publisher's Clearing House sweepstakes or something?"

"Louise!"

"All right, I'll be serious," she said with a smile. "What's happened that's so great?"

"I got it!" Caitlin grinned. Then, all at once, her happiness was too much. Standing up, she whirled happily around the room. "I got the job in Boston!"

"Hey, that really is terrific." Louise forced enthusiasm into her voice. "Have you told Julian yet?"

"I'll tell him when I see him tonight. I'm meeting him for an early dinner at—" She glanced at the clock radio beside her bed. "Oh, my gosh, I'm going to be late. I'm supposed to be meeting him in fifteen minutes, and I wanted to take a shower," she said. "Oh, well, I guess just changing will have to do."

"You know, I really envy you," Louise said, watching Caitlin as she quickly pulled off her clothes, placing them neatly beside the pile of books she'd brought back from the library. "I mean, getting to go off to Boston. I wish I'd been able to find a great job like that. Then I wouldn't have to go home to Connecticut."

"Oh, Louise," Caitlin said, pausing in front of her closet. She took out a pair of dark green cotton slacks, looked at them, and put them back in the closet. "Are things still awful at home?"

"That's putting it mildly. I don't think my parents are ever going to stop fighting. And now that my sister's living at home with her little boy—well, I'd give anything not to have to spend the summer there."

"That's really too bad," Caitlin sympathized. As she dressed in a white straight skirt and a pale yellow top, she thought to herself that Louise wasn't alone in having problems at home. She wasn't looking forward to spending more than a month at home watching Colin Wollman fawning all over her grandmother and Nicole Wollman hanging on her father.

"You don't suppose you'd like to pack me in your suitcase and take me to Boston with you?" Louise suggested half seriously.

"Sorry, I don't think you'd fit," Caitlin replied. She slipped her feet into white canvas sandals and went over to the dresser to do her hair. As she picked up her brush, she had an idea. "Hey," she said, turning to face Louise, "I do have an idea, though. How would you like to spend at least one month away from Connecticut?"

Louise's face lit up. "How?" she asked.

"You could come to Ryan Acres with me. I'm going to be staying there through the end of June. We could have a lot of fun. Riding, playing tennis, swimming. Then, when it's time for me to leave for Boston, I could drive you home. After all, Hartford's on the way."

"Oh, Caitlin, that sounds fabulous!" Louise hesitated. "But what about your grandmother? Wouldn't she be upset if you brought a guest home for more than a month?"

"No," Caitlin assured her. "My grandmother's used to having guests. The house is loaded with bedrooms. There's plenty of room."

"You're sure?"

"Absolutely." Caitlin smiled and then glanced down at her watch. "We can figure out the details later. Right now I've really got to run. I don't want to keep Julian waiting." Picking up her straw bag, she slipped the leather straps over her shoulder and walked to the door. Then she paused and turned back to Louise. "I really think it will be fun!"

Yes, Louise thought when Caitlin had gone. She would have fun. Even though she would have to spend the entire time continuing to pretend that she was Caitlin's best friend, it would be worth it. A whole month away from her family! And she'd be staying at an estate like Ryan Acres, too! With a satisfied smile, she unfolded her legs and stood up.

But one of her legs had fallen asleep, and she lost her balance, falling against Caitlin's bed. The bump jarred the bed, and a book from the pile Caitlin had left there fell to the floor.

As she bent to pick it up, Louise recognized the book. It was one of those dreary philosophy books Caitlin was always borrowing from Julian. She started to put the book back on the bed when she noticed the edge of a folded piece of paper sticking out from it. Curiosity got the better of her, and she pulled it from the book. *It's probably just some notes Caitlin made,* she thought. Still, she opened the folded sheet of paper and began to read. It was a letter to Julian from his mother. What Louise read completely astonished her.

> You know how proud I am of you for getting that job with that doctor in Boston. I wish you could come to Rock Ridge for a visit because I'm afraid it will be your last chance to see your father alive. He's doing so poorly. The visiting nurse said the sickness has ruined most of his lungs. He has such trouble breathing.

Louise's hands dropped to her lap, still holding the letter. "I don't believe it!" she exclaimed. She looked at the date of the letter. It had been written a week earlier. The writing was poor, as if the writer of the letter wasn't used to putting words on paper. Frowning slightly, Louise refolded the letter.

Obviously Julian had forgotten he had put the letter in the book. It was obvious, too, that Caitlin didn't know it was there. If she had, she would have taken it straight to Julian—or Jake, as his mother called him. *Was Jake his nickname?* she wondered. Was using it an affectation—a name to impress people with? A sly smile touched Louise's lips. *Julian is a miner's son. Who would believe it? Oh, this is priceless.*

71

Suddenly Louise laughed out loud. Regina Ryan really would have a fit if she knew her precious granddaughter was in love with the son of a poor miner dying of black lung disease!

Louise stood up and walked over to her dresser. Opening the jewelry box that sat on top, she reached in and pulled out a tray, revealing a secret compartment. She put the letter into it, then replaced the tray and closed the box. *There*, she thought with satisfaction. She would keep secret her newfound knowledge about Julian until she could use it to her advantage.

Caitlin told Julian her good news as she slid happily into his arms at his apartment. He hugged her tightly and laughed happily. "See, I told you there wasn't anything to worry about. There's no one else who could possibly be more qualified than you. This calls for a celebration! Let's drive up to Roberto's," Julian suggested.

"I'm not really hungry anymore," Caitlin replied. "I guess the excitement of getting the job made me lose my appetite."

"Well, then, maybe a little exercise would help." They left Julian's apartment and walked through a little park that bordered the village.

An hour later, after the sky had turned dark and starry, they crossed into the village and entered a small pizza shop.

They were halfway through a sausage pan pizza when Caitlin mentioned that she had asked Louise to come to Ryan Acres for the month of June. As she paused to take another bite of the slice in her hand, she looked over at Julian. She was surprised to see he was frowning.

"Julian? What's the matter?"

"Hmm," Julian answered distractedly, continuing to scowl. *Why did Caitlin invite Louise to Ryan Acres?* he fumed silently. He had just begun to breathe easily again, knowing that soon Louise would not be around to spoil his plans. And if anyone could ruin all of his hard work, it was Louise. He had used her jealousy of Caitlin to enlist her help in destroying Caitlin and Jed's relationship, but Louise didn't know the full extent of his plot, and she might easily give away vital information in the reassuring atmosphere of Ryan Acres. Then again, she might say something to Caitlin just to spite him. After all, he had led her on and used her.

"Julian!" Caitlin repeated, leaning toward him.

Her voice snapped him out of his daydreaming. Seeing the concerned expression on her face, he realized how angry he must have looked. "I'm sorry, Caitlin," he apologized. "I suddenly remembered a problem at the lab," he lied. "It just occurred to me that there might be further complications."

"Oh, that's too bad."

"Well, that's science for you." He shrugged and forced himself to smile. "But I don't want to think about work now. We're still celebrating your new job, right?"

"Right,"Caitlin said, smiling back at him.

"Then how about finishing our pizza and going to a movie? There's a good one playing at the Village Cinema." He glanced at the clock over the register. "I think we just have time to make it."

"Great! Can we get popcorn, too? Would you believe that I'm still hungry."

"Popcorn, too. With lots of melted butter." Arm in arm, they left the pizzeria.

9

"You know, there are only two things I really hate about college," Louise remarked to Caitlin. She was sitting cross-legged in the middle of their room, surrounded by half-filled cardboard boxes. Her cotton shorts and tank top were smudged with dirt and dust, and her long blond hair was pulled back in a ponytail.

"I know, don't tell me," Caitlin replied sympathetically. "One is unpacking when you arrive in the fall, and the other is packing back up in the spring."

"How did you ever guess?" Louise glanced enviously at Caitlin's side of the room. The shelves were empty, and a stack of neatly packed boxes was pushed against one wall. "I can't believe you're finished already."

"Well, if it's any consolation," Caitlin said as she zipped up the lavender sun dress she had just slipped over her head, "I felt exactly the same way yesterday when I was packing all my stuff." She nodded toward the boxes on her side of the room. "But I knew I had to do it. Rollins, my grandmother's chauffeur, is coming to pick it all up today. Besides, if I hadn't gotten it finished, I wouldn't have time to go shopping with Julian this afternoon."

"Oh, I know. It's just that you always seem so organized," Louise commented. She leaned her elbows on her knees and looked at the small stuffed bear she was swinging in one hand. "I'm just a terrible packer. I can't seem to make up my mind about the simplest things—like whether to keep this bear or not. I suppose I should keep it for sentimental reasons. Yancy won it for me at the carnival. But then, I'm not going with Yancy anymore. You know what I mean?"

"Yes," Caitlin said. "I know exactly what you mean." She slipped a pair of navy flats onto her bare feet. Her legs were already tan from two months of running and playing tennis. "If I have any doubts about whether or not to get rid of something, I don't. You can always throw it away later if you decide you don't want it."

"That makes sense." Louise tossed the bear into the box of things she was going to keep. She picked up a stack of used notebooks, glanced briefly at them, and tossed them into a large trash bag.

"By the way, is there anything you want Rollins to take with him to Ryan Acres when he picks up my stuff?" Caitlin asked Louise as she pulled her long dark hair back and tied it with a lavender ribbon. "Since we're driving in my car, there'll only be room for a couple of suitcases each."

"I don't think so," Louise replied, looking around at the various piles of clothes and books on her bed. "I just have two suitcases to take to your place. My dad and mom are coming for all my junk tomorrow morning—if I ever finish packing, that is." She made a face.

"Well, if you're not done by the time I get back, I'll help you," Caitlin offered.

"What are you going shopping for anyway?"

"Julian wants to buy some new shirts to take to Boston. He wants to make a good impression on Dr. Kramer."

"Hmmm. It sounds like quite a domestic little outing," Louise said.

"Oh, come on, Louise," Caitlin objected. But in spite of her casual denial, the idea of the shopping trip did please Caitlin. She picked up her purse and looked at Louise. "Do you want me to bring you anything from town?"

"No, thanks," Louise replied in her most pitiful voice. "You go on and have a good time. Don't think about poor little me for a minute."

"Oh, Louise, you're too much," Caitlin said, shaking her head and laughing at her roommate's sad but funny expression. "Tell you what, I'll bring you back a present." Then she added in a teasing voice, "But you'll only get it if you've finished all your packing!" With that, Caitlin left the room and headed for the elevator.

On her way through the lobby, Caitlin stopped to get her mail. There was a piece of junk mail, which she immediately tossed into the nearby trash basket. There was also a letter from her old friend, Emily Michaels, a high school senior at Highgate.

Emily was one of Caitlin's closest friends from her days at the academy, and she was also Jed's cousin. Caitlin had not heard from Emily since Thanksgiving. Caitlin guessed that Emily had kept her distance because she was very close to Jed, and she didn't want to appear to take sides. *But then why was she writing now?* Caitlin wondered.

She looked thoughtfully at the envelope in her hand, tapping it against her fingers. She wanted to open it, but in a way she was afraid. Glancing at her watch, she realized that she still had a few minutes before Julian was supposed to arrive. Caitlin hesitated only a second more, and then turning the envelope over, she ripped open the flap. It was an invitation of some kind, Caitlin realized, as she pulled out another envelope. Inside was a formal invitation on heavy, cream-colored paper. As Caitlin pulled it out of the envelope, some folded sheets of notepaper, which had been tucked into the invitation, fell to the floor. She quickly picked up the note, and read the engraved words.

Mr. and Mrs. Lorin C. Michaels
cordially invite you
to a party in honor of
the engagement
of their daughter
Emily Anne Michaels
to
James Wentworth Kent III
June 28th at two p.m.
RSVP

Emily was engaged! Caitlin couldn't believe it. She was only a high school senior. Emily was much too young to be getting married. Then Caitlin shook her head. Hadn't Louise just accused her and Julian of being domestic? *Why not Emily?* she asked herself. *She's only a year younger.* Caitlin looked at the invitation again. It made everything so formal, so permanent. But then, she thought of herself and Julian as a permanent couple, didn't she?

Quickly Caitlin unfolded the note Emily had enclosed and began to read. She was dying to find out who James Wentworth Kent III was.

Dear Caitlin,
Well, I'm pretty sure that you've looked at the invitation by now and just about fallen over. I'm still feeling a little dazed myself. Everything has happened so fast. I met Jim this winter when I

went to college at Brown. Did I tell you I
graduated early and got into Brown? Actually, it
was because of family connections. Well, anyway, Jim surprised me with the most gorgeous
diamond ring on the first day of spring, two
months after we met. Isn't that romantic! It was
tied to the ribbon on a huge bouquet of flowers.
I know, I know—we're too young and impul-
sive.

Of course my mom wasn't too thrilled but
decided that we had to have a party anyway, so
I'm sending you the enclosed. They're straight
off the press. I know the party isn't for a month,
but I wanted to make sure everyone would be
there. Who knows where all our old friends
from Highgate will be for the summer.

A tiny jolt of terror suddenly shot through
Caitlin. *Will Jed be at the party, too? Probably*, she
thought. Taking a deep breath, Caitlin looked
back at the letter.

I'm sure you're dying to know all about Jim, so
here goes. As I told you, I met him here at
Brown. He's a senior, incredibly adorable, and
also incredibly smart. He's going into business
with his father after graduation right here in
town. They're marble importers, so we'll get to
go to Europe pretty often.

We're planning to get married in the fall. Can
you believe it, Caitlin? I'm getting married!! Oh,
I know you're probably worried that I'm not
going to finish college, but you're wrong. I'm
going to stay at Brown and be a wife at the same
time. I can't imagine waiting three more years—

I hate being away from Jim even for a day as it is. I want to be with him every second. Love really is wonderful!!

Caitlin smiled briefly. As if she didn't know about love!

Caitlin, I'm not sure how you're going to feel about this, but I want you to know that Jed will probably be coming to the party. My parents have invited him to spend a couple of weeks here, too. I just wanted to let you know so you'd be prepared. I invited Melanie, too, but she's going on a bike tour in Europe with a group of her friends. It was a graduation present from her father.

I know this is none of my business, Caitlin, and I've told myself I should just stay out of it because I care so much about both you and Jed, but I have to admit that I've never quite understood the reason you two broke up. Jed would only say that things fell apart because you two were so far away from each other. Whatever it was, I have to tell you that I'm absolutely sure that Jed isn't seeing Eve or anyone else, at least not in a romantic way. Don't let her presence out there in Montana keep you apart—if that's what broke you up. I'm sorry if I've butted in where I don't belong, but I can't help wanting to see you two together again.

I'll see you soon, and I hope we'll have a chance to really talk then.

Love,
Emily

Slowly Caitlin refolded the letter and put it back into the envelope, along with the invitation. She thought about what Emily had said about Jed. Emily probably honestly believed that he wasn't involved with Eve. Unfortunately, Emily was almost too nice. She always wanted to see the rosy side of any situation. No, Jed and Eve were seeing each other all right. There was no doubt in Caitlin's mind about that. Caitlin stuffed the letter into her purse and snapped it shut.

"Caitlin! Is something the matter?" Julian's voice surprised her. She hadn't seen him come up behind her.

"Oh, Julian," she said, forcing a smile. "Nothing's the matter. Why do you ask?"

"Well, I saw you put that letter in your purse. From the look on your face, I thought it might be bad news."

"No, no." She decided there was no use telling him about Emily's engagement party and the possibility of her seeing Jed. It would just upset Julian. The last thing he needed to think about while he was in Boston was Caitlin's going to a party that her ex-boyfriend would be attending as well. "It was just a letter from an old friend from high school. She reminded me of old times, and I guess I got a little nostalgic."

"Sad times?"

"No, actually her letter was pretty upbeat. It's

that those days are over and I miss my old friends." Giving a little shake of her head, Caitlin smiled up at Julian. She took his arm and headed toward the door. "But I don't want to dwell in the past any longer. It's an absolutely gorgeous day, and I want to spend as much of it as I can with you."

"Then we went out for Chinese food," she told Louise several hours later. Kicking off her sandals, she wiggled her toes. "I must have walked ten miles today."

"Well, I stayed here and finished packing. Hey, where's my present?" Louise looked at Caitlin expectantly.

Caitlin reached for one of the smaller bags she had dumped next to her when she had plopped down on the bed. "When I make a promise, I keep it." She opened the bag and took out a small square box wrapped in gold paper. "Here you go," she said as she handed the box to Louise.

"Oh, you're a mind reader!" Louise exclaimed. "Godiva chocolates are my favorites." She opened the box of candy, took one, and popped it in her mouth. "Want one?" she asked, holding the box out to Caitlin.

"No, thanks. I'm still stuffed from all that Chinese food." Remembering something, she reached for her purse. "I brought you another little present, too." She took a small cellophane package out of her purse and tossed it to Louise.

"Fortune cookies. What fun! I hope I get a good one. I believe them, you know"— Louise tore open the package and took one out—"at least if the fortune turns out to be a good one." She broke open the cookie and unfolded the slip of paper that had been inside.

"Well?" Caitlin asked. "What does it say?"

"It's a good one! Listen to this. 'A handsome man will soon enter your life.'" Louise glanced at Caitlin. "Do you know anyone at Ryan Acres who fits that description?"

"Well, let's see," Caitlin replied, her eyes twinkling. "There's Rollins. And Barnes, the gardener," Caitlin replied, stifling a laugh. "They're very nice, but I think they're both a little old for you."

"Oh, well. You can't have everything," Louise said philosophically. She began to laugh, too.

10

Sunlight filtered down through the branches hanging over the surface of the small pond. The light made dots, like gold coins, on the water. Caitlin and Julian were sitting on the grassy bank near the edge. Julian's arms were draped casually about Caitlin's shoulders, and she was comfortably curled up against him. Her head was nestled into the curve between his shoulder and chest. Behind them, farther up on the bank, a red- and white-checked picnic cloth was spread out, and on it were the remains of their lunch—a torn loaf of french bread, a leftover wedge of Brie, and the stems from a carton of strawberries. Caitlin broke the long, easy silence.

"This afternoon has been so perfect. I wish it could go on and on forever."

"I wish it could, too," Julian replied, gently rubbing his cheek against the silky softness of her hair. "I have to admit that I'm really excited about leaving for Boston tomorrow and starting my work with Dr. Kramer. I'm more excited about it than I've ever been about anything to do with my career." He kissed the top of her head lightly. "But, at the same time, I can't bear the idea of being separated from you for a whole month."

"Oh, Julian, I know," Caitlin murmured, snuggling even closer against him. "I wish it were already July and we were both together in Boston."

"Hmmm, yes," Julian agreed, his voice low and warm in her ear. *Together in my apartment*, he thought, tightening his hand where it cupped her arm. Yes, he, too, wished the month were over because then he could finally sleep with Caitlin, finally possess her completely. And then he would crush her with the knowledge that she'd given herself to a man who was the son of one of her grandmother's miners—a man who wanted to see her hurt and cheapened.

Father. Thoughts of the middle-aged man who looked thirty years older than he was because of his years of hard, dirty work in the coal mines came surging into Julian's mind. He remembered the letter his mother had written him recently, how she had pleaded for him to come home for a visit because his father was near death. Well, his father had been near death for almost two years, lying there in a bedroom, coughing his life away. Why would he go back to Rock Ridge to see that?

And even if his father died, what did it matter? Julian only felt badly about how much it would hurt his mother. He and his father had never been close. Well, perhaps they had been when he was very young, before he became old enough to realize that his father's job in the mines was responsible for the poverty they lived in. Even then, his father had been too sick to work a full shift at the mine. And the small amount of money he brought home had to be stretched to take care of them all.

He could almost remember the exact day that he had decided it would be his gift for learning that would allow him to someday leave Rock Ridge. Since then, he had worked hard, eventually getting his scholarship to Carleton Hill. And all the while his father had continued to tell him that he was just wasting his time. He said it even now. It was too bad that he wouldn't live long enough to see his son become a doctor.

Julian envisioned the day he'd become a doctor, and his heart began to pound as it always did. His career in medicine was the only thing in his life that meant more to him than ruining Caitlin Ryan. He had promised himself that he would rise above his shabby beginnings, and Julian knew that he could never go back on that promise—no matter the cost. And once he'd made it, he would send for his little sister, Kathy. He would bring her to live with him and see that she went to the best schools. He would make sure that her life wasn't wasted in Rock Ridge.

Julian knew his brother was smart, too. But Will had neither the burning ambition that he had, nor the bright spark of intelligence that he saw in Kathy. In a way, Kathy was very much like Caitlin—

What's the matter with me? Julian asked himself. He just couldn't allow himself to think that way—to compare Kathy to Caitlin. It was too dangerous. He hated Caitlin! Hatred was the only emotion he could ever allow himself to feel toward her.

But when she's here in my arms . . . Julian gently turned Caitlin so she faced him. He looked at her for a long moment, seeing two small reflections of himself in the brilliant blue of her eyes. *Why? Why does she have to be so beautiful, so desirable?*

He brushed his hand gently against her cheek. Then with his hand cupping her chin, he tilted her face upward. His kiss was slow and light at first, but it grew stronger. Julian circled his arm around her waist, pulling her to him. Caitlin melted into his arms, returning his kiss.

When their lips parted, Julian trailed a line of tender kisses over her chin and down her neck. Then he turned his head, and buried his face in the thick mass of hair that fell across her shoulder. "Oh, Caitlin," he said in a low voice. "I can't bear to think I won't be able to hold you like this for an entire month."

"Oh, Julian, I love you so." Her voice was shaky with emotion.

"And I love you, too, Caitlin." He moved his head away from hers so that he was again looking into her eyes. Her eyes were dark, filled with tender longing.

For a brief moment Julian thought about making love to Caitlin then and there, on the private grassy slope of the pond's edge. But he stopped himself. It wasn't the time nor the place. He must wait until they got to Boston.

Gently he pushed her away from him and smiled. "It's getting late, Caitlin. I still have some packing to do, and my bus leaves tomorrow morning at six."

"Just a little while longer," she pleaded. Then her face brightened. "I could drive you to the station so we could have more time together."

"No, Caitlin," Julian argued softly. "I told you, I hate to say goodbye in public places. I want to remember you here, not standing in the middle of a bus station."

"Julian, I don't care where we are. Being with you is always better than being apart—no matter what we're doing or where we are."

"Caitlin, I mean it." His voice was still low, but

firm. "Now, let's get going. It's a long drive back." He helped her up, then he bent his head and kissed her again. But this time he did not let the kiss become heated. They walked back toward Caitlin's car hand in hand, Julian carrying the picnic basket.

On the drive back, both of them were silent, absorbed in their own thoughts. Later that afternoon Caitlin pulled into the driveway beside Julian's small apartment. Julian leaned toward her, but before he could give her a final kiss, she stopped him. "Wait, I have something for you. A graduation present." She opened her purse and took out a long slender box. "I know I should wait until graduation, but since you're not going to the ceremony, I decided to give it to you now. Congratulations." Smiling proudly, she handed him the small white box tied with a narrow silver ribbon. "It's really a very traditional present, but I think you'll like it anyway."

"I don't know what to say," Julian said in surprise. It hadn't even occurred to him that anyone would give him a graduation present. Certainly he knew he wouldn't get anything from his parents. He looked at the box and then at Caitlin. "Thank you. That's the most thoughtful thing anyone's ever done for me."

"Open it," she urged in an excited voice.

Julian slid the ribbon off the box, then lifted off

the lid. Nestled inside was a gold Mark Cross pen.

"Look at what I had engraved on it," Caitlin said, biting her lower lip.

Picking the pen up, Julian turned it so that he could see the engraved lettering against the gold finish of the pen. It read: Julian Stokes, M.D.

"I know I won't be able to call you doctor for a few years, but I thought it would make you feel good to have this with you. You know, through all of those long hours of labs and exams." She reached over and touched his arm lovingly.

"Caitlin, I really don't know what to say." He turned the pen around in his fingers, staring at it.

"Just say that you love me," she replied with a smile. "And that you like the pen, of course."

"I love it!" he exclaimed. Then the look in his eyes turned more serious. "And I love you, too. Oh, Caitlin, I'm going to miss you so much. I'll call you as often as I can, and we can write each other, too," Julian said. Looking into Caitlin's tear-filled eyes, he almost wanted to believe his words. It would have made such a touching scene if he'd really meant them.

"What will I do without you?" Caitlin asked as Julian leaned toward her to kiss her goodbye. A tear slid down her cheek.

"You'll be fine," Julian replied, pulling her into his arms and kissing her tenderly. "Just remember how much I adore you and that we'll be together in only four weeks." With that, he pulled away from her and opened the door. Grabbing the picnic basket, he got out of the car. He waved at Caitlin, who was now crying openly, and turned quickly away. Caitlin watched as he walked to his door, unlocked it, and went inside.

11

Jed drove down the highway with his left arm
resting on the edge of the open window. His
hand was curled lightly up over the top of the
pickup's cab. The sun had already tanned his
arm.

Eve sat beside Jed, her position almost the
same as his except that she had one booted foot
across her knee. She wasn't wearing her seat
belt. When Jed had suggested she buckle up, her
answer had been flip. "Hey, just living is taking a
chance. If we crash, we crash. I'd rather be
comfortable than worry about dying all the
time."

That statement was typical of Eve and her way
of thinking, Jed thought idly as he stared out at
the straight, deserted road. Eve never planned
ahead. That morning, for instance, if she hadn't
bumped into him, she might still be sitting in her
dorm trying to figure out how she was going to
get herself and her stuff the hundred and eighty

miles to the Towerses' ranch, which neighbored the Michaelses' place. Fortunately she'd found him just as he was about to leave. He was outside his dorm, putting the last of his stuff in the back of the pickup.

"I thought you were supposed to have a ride with a girlfriend," Jed had said when she asked if he had room for her and some of her things.

"Yeah, I thought so, too," she answered, shrugging. "But when I went to find her, she'd already left school. There was some mix-up, I guess." *A carefully planned mix-up*, she thought smugly as Jed had helped her into the pickup. Then they drove to her dorm to pick up her things.

"Tell you what," she said after he had loaded her luggage into the truck, "I'll treat you to breakfast at Benny's if you want to wait and get gas in Bozeman. I'm starved."

That had been a little over an hour before. They'd gone to Benny's after filling up the tank. She'd insisted he get steak and eggs, even telling the waitress exactly how he liked his steak. Then she had ordered only coffee and toast for herself. *Girls*, Jed thought. Sometimes he really didn't understand them.

"Thanks again for breakfast," he said now as he drove. "I really appreciated it."

"Sure." She paused. "Was the steak really

okay? I mean, it was a Benny's steak, but you never can tell."

"It was fine."

"Just the way you like it? I know you like your steaks medium-rare."

"It was great, all right?" He took his eyes off the road long enough to give her a smile. "Well, maybe not great, but okay." He returned his attention to the road.

Eve continued to look at Jed's profile. She began to think about the summer ahead, about the time she would spend with him. Eve was determined to do everything in her power to make Jed forget Caitlin Ryan. She smiled, thinking about the daring new bikini she had just bought. After Jed had seen her in it, he wouldn't keep thinking about that spoiled society brat. And then there were the barbecue parties Eve would throw. She thought of herself and Jed dancing under a romantic summer moon. Yes, give her the summer with Jed, and Caitlin would be nothing but a faded memory—if that.

Jed's thoughts had been including Caitlin also. He was thinking about the invitation he had received from his cousin, Emily, to come to Virginia for her engagement party. In the letter that had come with the invitation, Emily mentioned that she had invited Caitlin. The second he had read that Caitlin would be there, Jed knew he had to be at that party to talk to Caitlin face to face. If they could do that, Jed was certain they could smooth out their differences. He would make her see that he was the only one for her and that this other guy was just someone she had turned to for sympathy.

Jed frowned. He still didn't know exactly why they *had* split up. Sure, it wasn't an ideal situation being separated for the school year. And they had had misunderstandings, too. But those things alone shouldn't have destroyed their relationship. No, it was something more. Her letters to him had been strange, her jealousy of Eve was almost irrational. It was as if somehow she wanted to believe the worst about him and Eve. But why would Caitlin feel that way? It didn't make sense. Jed shook his head. Soon he was going to straighten this whole mess out. Yes, he just needed to see Caitlin, and everything would be fine. His frown faded, and Jed smiled. He would get Caitlin back. And then nothing, or no one, would ever separate them again.

"I got a letter from my cousin Emily the other day," he told Eve. "She's getting married, and she's invited Melanie and me to her engagement party at the end of the month. Melanie can't go, but I'm planning to go, maybe even spend a couple of weeks there."

"What?" Eve gasped in surprise. She couldn't believe her ears. It was obvious that he was really jumping at the chance to go to Virginia because that was where Caitlin would be. Quickly Eve tried to think of how she could convince him not to go. "But, Jed, how can you take time off to go all the way to Virginia just for a party?" Eve asked, recovering smoothly. "What about the ranch? I thought you promised your father you were going to stay in Montana and work on the ranch for the summer. There's so much to do now."

"Look, I'll only be gone for two weeks," Jed argued. "After that, my father will have my full attention for the rest of the summer." He paused, and when he spoke again, his voice had an edge to it. "The way I see it, I've just given my father a whole year by going to Montana Agricultural College instead of going East to study law the way I had planned. Well, now it's my turn to do what I want. In fact, I've already re-enrolled at Carleton Hill. As much as I love my father, I have to live my life my way. I'm going back to Virginia to study law with or without my father's blessing," he explained, adding silently, *with or without Caitlin's blessing, too*. "You do understand, don't you, Eve?"

"I suppose so," Eve replied, trying to sound as if she agreed. What else could she do? If she argued with him, it might drive Jed away. No, she had to be sympathetic. "So, when are you planning to leave?"

"As soon as I can. But depending on how things are going at the ranch, it might be more than a week or two before I can leave."

"Do you think your father's going to object to your leaving so soon?" Eve asked. She hoped his father would put his foot down and tell Jed he couldn't go.

"I honestly don't know," Jed replied. "But it won't make any difference. I've made up my mind, and I'm going. But I do want a chance to convince my father of how important this trip is to me."

Important! The word, and the way Jed had said it, stung Eve deeply. *Translate important to mean Caitlin*, she thought. *Darn that Caitlin Ryan!* As she thought about Caitlin, a bitter look crossed Eve's face. She turned away from Jed and looked out the window. *When will thoughts of that girl ever leave Jed?*

Two thousand miles away Caitlin was also heading home from college. She was driving her red Nissan 280ZX along the interstate, Louise next to her. A rock tape was playing on the cassette deck.

With the loud music, there was no sense in trying to talk, but Louise didn't mind. She was happy to just sit back, close her eyes, and enjoy the ride. Louise opened her eyes as the tape ended. She looked around, surprised to see that they'd turned off the highway and were now driving along a sunny country road. Rolling fields spread out on either side of the road, and Louise noticed that some of them were sectioned off by white, wooden paddock fences.

"It's not much farther," Caitlin said. Removing the tape, she put the cassette on the dashboard and picked up another. Glancing briefly at the title, she flipped it into the slot. The quieter sounds of Billy Joel began to play. "As you can see, this is mostly horse country. I think we have about the best pastureland in the country. Maybe even better than Kentucky's." She smiled at Louise. "I'm glad you ride."

"Yes. But this is so different from Connecticut," Louise said, glancing around. "Connecticut is so crowded, and this is so open."

"Well, we love to hunt. And you need a lot of open space for that."

As she spoke Caitlin turned onto another, narrower road. After a few hundred feet, she turned again, this time to enter a private drive. A border of magnificent oaks, each at least a hundred years old, arched over the drive in a natural canopy of green. White-fenced paddocks, enclosing grazing thoroughbreds, also ran alongside the drive. As they came out from beneath the trees, the drive curved around a broad expanse of manicured lawn at the center of which was a fountain and reflecting pool, surrounded by perfectly manicured flower beds. A two-century-old, white-columned Virginia manor house stood before them. Louise drew in her breath at the sight as Caitlin brought the car to a halt beside the stone front steps. Immediately one of the impressive double doors opened and Rollins, the portly, middle-aged man who served as both butler and chauffeur, came out of the house and started down to meet them. As he did, Caitlin turned to Louise. "Welcome to Ryan Acres."

12

Louise finished smoothing sun tan lotion on her leg. Then, recapping the tube, she dropped it to the flagstone pool deck. "Oh, this is heaven," she said and sank back against the plump cushions of the chaise longue.

"Mmm, you're right," Caitlin murmured sleepily from her own nearby chaise. "Just think, no more exams or classes or homework for three whole months."

"You said it," Louise agreed. But the end of classes wasn't what she had meant was heavenly. Leaning her head back so that none of her face was in shadow, she closed her eyes against the sun. She had been at Ryan Acres for three days, and she was still in awe of the estate.

And it wasn't as if she were poor. After all, her family's home near Hartford was one of the most elegant homes in the area. And they had a pool, too. Of course it wasn't so large as the one at Ryan Acres. And Ryan Acres did have tennis courts and private stables, which were larger than those at the public place where Louise rode at home. But it was the grounds that were the most magnificent—manicured velvet green lawns and perpetually blooming flower beds.

Louise still hadn't figured out exactly how many servants Mrs. Ryan had, but she knew there were four in the main house—Rollins, two maids and a cook. Then there were gardeners and stable hands. She wrinkled her nose as she thought of her mother bragging about their "jewel of a housekeeper." The woman couldn't even be considered a proper servant. She refused to wear a uniform of any kind, and she insisted on calling Mrs. Bates by her first name. No, staying at Ryan Acres was truly living. Louise decided she could be perfectly happy staying there forever.

She opened her eyes long enough to glance in Caitlin's direction. Caitlin was lying on her stomach, head pillowed in her arms. She looked as if she were asleep. Louise thought about her roommate. Caitlin had spent much of the school year on campus, only returning home for Christmas, spring break, and a few weekends. What was she trying to avoid? What would keep her away from that fantastic estate?

Of course Mrs. Ryan didn't seem as though she would be easy to live with. She was definitely cool. She put on a big welcoming act when they had arrived, but Louise noticed the same appraising look in Mrs. Ryan's eyes that she'd seen in the eyes of some of her mother's friends. It was as if she were being added up, point by socially important point.

And Louise had no idea what to make of Mrs. Ryan's friend, Colin Wollman. She had been told he was the Ryan Mining lawyer, but she was also sure there was more to it than that. He was hovering next to Mrs. Ryan constantly. Louise thought he was handsome, for someone in his forties, but he was sort of—well—too slick. He might be Mrs. Ryan's attorney, but he acted as if their relationship was much more personal.

But that couldn't be right, either. Because how could he explain that little scene she had nearly walked in on earlier that afternoon? That had certainly been interesting! She had started to walk into the library, thinking it was the game room where Caitlin was waiting for her, when she saw Colin with his arms around a gorgeous blond woman. Louise could have sworn he had been about to kiss her, but at the last second, the blond had whispered something into his ear and he moved quickly over to close the door. Was he putting the move on both Mrs. Ryan and the blond? Louise decided to keep what she had seen to herself, in case she could use it to some advantage later. But she wondered just how much Caitlin knew about what was going on.

"Caitlin!" Louise said and rolled over onto her side so she was facing her roommate. She leaned on one elbow.

Caitlin opened her eyes. "What?" she asked, looking sleepily at Louise.

"Who was that pretty blond woman who came to see Mr. Wollman after lunch? His secretary?"

"Hardly," Caitlin replied with a sour look. "That's Nicole Wollman, Colin's sister."

"Sister?" *Well, well,* Louise thought, *that's interesting.* "Funny, she doesn't look much like him," Louise went on. "I mean they don't even have the same coloring."

"I guess that happens sometimes," Caitlin answered casually. But she remembered how that was the first thing that had struck her about Nicole and Colin when she'd been introduced to them. And, it had caused her some very strong suspicions. Maybe someday she would find out exactly what their relationship was, but right then she just wanted to forget about the Wollmans. She was in too good a mood, and thinking about Nicole always gave her a headache. She started to close her eyes again.

But Louise wanted to know more. "Do I gather from the face you made that you're not exactly thrilled with the gorgeous Ms. Wollman?"

"You got that very right." With a resigned

sigh, Caitlin pulled herself up to sit cross-legged, facing Louise. "She's a cheap little flirt, and she's been chasing my father for almost a year now. It makes me absolutely furious that he can't see through her. Especially considering how transparent she is. I can't even stand being in the same room with that woman. And when I see her with my father, I want to scream and—and—"

"Maybe scratch her eyes out?" Louise suggested.

"Something like that," Caitlin said, suddenly laughing.

Louise nodded. With such a colorful cast of characters, she was sure that her stay at Ryan Acres was going to be better than watching a soap opera.

"But," Caitlin said, leaning forward, her elbows on her knees, "let's stop talking about Nicole. I want to tell you about my father. He's coming over this afternoon so you'll finally have a chance to meet him." Caitlin looked happy. "Maybe I'm prejudiced, but I think he's wonderful."

"Well, I know he's good-looking, that's for sure. At least he is in that photograph you kept on your desk at school."

"He's even better-looking in person," Caitlin replied proudly. "And he's kind and thoughtful, too. That's what makes him such a good doctor."

"Didn't you say he works for some hospital?"

"Yes. He's the director at Meadow Valley Hospital. It's a very well-respected smallish clinic."

"I thought I remembered it was something like that. Is he coming here to dinner?" Louise was wondering if they were going to be dressing formally again. Apparently everyone dressed up a lot at Ryan Acres. Louise wished that Caitlin had said something about it when she was packing her clothes. She was going to have to buy some new clothes if they kept on having formal dinners.

"I'm not sure," Caitlin said. "When he called, all he said was that he was coming over because he had a surprise for me. I guess he'll stay for dinner."

"Hmmm, that sounds exciting. Do you think it might be something big—like a new car?"

"No," Caitlin replied, shaking her head. "Actually, it sounded more like he had some news to tell me."

"Ahhh." Louise nodded. "Then maybe he wants to give you a trip. Maybe to Paris or Rome!"

Caitlin smiled. "I hardly think so. My father knows my summer's already taken up with my job in Boston."

"Oh, well, what kind of news do you suppose it is, then?"

"I don't know. Whatever it is, I'm sure I'll love it," Caitlin said happily.

"So, Nicole, just when is Gordon going to spring the news on Caitlin?" Colin asked. They were standing by the library window, watching Caitlin and Louise as they talked by the pool.

"This afternoon," Nicole replied. Her gaze was centered on Caitlin, assessing her. It had been a few months since she had seen her, and although she hated to admit it, Caitlin was definitely a beautiful woman. She was only eighteen, but the past year in college had given her a sophistication of someone much older. It was the way she held herself, the way she moved. And those classic features. No wonder Gordon was so proud of her. Nicole's eyes narrowed. Well, a lot of good her beauty would do her, she thought. Nicole smiled, knowing she held all the cards. She turned to face Colin. "Gordon will be over in about an hour."

"How do you think Caitlin will take his news?"

Nicole's ruby lips twisted into a cruel grin. "She's going to positively hate it when Gordon tells her that he and I are planning to be married."

A small muscle at the side of Colin's jaw tensed. "I'm not so sure I like the way you seem to be enjoying this. It's as if you really are looking forward to marrying Gordon Westlake."

"Oh, now, now, Colin." Nicole turned away from the window and placed a slender hand on his arm, looking up into his face. "Don't be that way. You're acting childish. You know he doesn't mean anything to me."

"I'm not being childish," Colin protested with a scowl. "I love you, Nicole. And it kills me to think about you going off on a honeymoon with that man."

"Then don't think about it," she replied breezily. She turned more serious. "*You're* the man I love, Colin. You've been so good this past year, pretending to care for that rich old witch Regina Ryan. You've got her eating out of your hand, and you've carried off your part of our plan beautifully. You're in a good enough position at Ryan Mining now that you can start funneling funds into the Swiss bank account that I'll be opening on my honeymoon. So, if you have to think about my honeymoon, just consider it a business trip." She smiled at him. "Okay?"

"I guess when you put it that way, it's all right."

"Of course it is, Colin. Besides, how do you think I've felt having to pretend that we're brother and sister, and all the time watching you play up to Regina?"

"Come on, Nicole. You said yourself that she's

an old woman. How do you think I felt spending my time with her when I'd much rather have been spending it with you?" Colin's voice grew husky. He bent toward her with the full intention of kissing her.

"Colin!" She stopped him, putting her hands against his chest. "Colin, you've really got to watch it. We almost got caught earlier today. I'm sure that friend of Caitlin's was snooping around when you started to kiss me before."

"Well, I can't help it. I'm getting impatient to get this over with."

"I know, I know." She nodded and patted his chest lovingly before dropping her hands away. "That's exactly why I'm rushing this wedding along. The quicker we get married, the quicker I'll get my hands on Gordon Westlake's money. As soon as I get back from the honeymoon, I'll file for divorce. Meanwhile, you handle your end of things at Ryan Mining. Then we'll dump the Ryan-Westlakes. It'll happen soon enough, I promise."

"And then, my darling, it will be a honeymoon for us." He smiled at her. "In warm, sunny South America."

"Ummm." Nicole returned his smile. "I can hardly wait."

13

Caitlin was too stunned to say anything. She could only sit and stare at her father. They were alone in the library. The walls of books, the dark mahogany paneling, the brocade drapes, and the heavy Aubusson carpet all seemed to magnify the silence that loomed between them. He was looking at her with hope. He knew Caitlin wouldn't be thrilled, but he wanted her to be happy for him. But she just couldn't be. She searched for something to say, anything that would convince him that what he was going to do was wrong.

"Caitlin?" Dr. Westlake asked, his voice a mixture of concern and confusion. "Don't you have anything to say, honey?"

"When?" she asked suddenly. "When is this thing going to take place?"

"*Thing?*" Dr. Westlake gave her a semi-amused look. "Caitlin, please try to be happy for me. At least, call it a wedding, not a thing."

"All right," Caitlin replied, drawing a deep breath, "when is your *wedding* going to take place?" *And please, please, Father,* she urged silently, *don't tell me "soon."*

"Sometime this summer."

"This summer!" Caitlin exclaimed in shock.

"Oh, I know you probably think that's a bit soon. But, darling, I've been seeing Nicole for a year now. It's not as if we need more time to get to know each other," Dr. Westlake explained reasonably. "I'm not exactly a teenager, you know. I'm almost middle-aged, and I want to start building a life with the woman I love."

"But—but what about me?" Caitlin asked in desperation, unable to think of anything else to say.

"Oh, Caitlin, nothing between us will change." His voice became tender. "The love I feel for you has nothing to do with my love for Nicole." He smiled at her. "Surely you must know the difference between those two kinds of love by now."

"Of course I do," Caitlin replied in exasperation.

"Then you must understand that I love both of you equally. Just because I'm marrying Nicole, it doesn't mean I love you any less," he said patiently.

Caitlin searched frantically for another argument. "Yes, you're right, Father. I do understand that kind of love," she finally said, nodding. "But what about my mother? Have you forgotten about her?"

"Laura." His voice was low, touched with the pain of remembering Caitlin's mother. "Oh, Caitlin," he said, "of course I haven't forgotten. And I never will. Your mother will always have a special place in my heart. But, Caitlin, we must all go on. Laura has been dead for more than eighteen years, and Nicole is the first woman I've been really serious about since then. Perhaps that's one reason I agreed with her when she suggested that it would be best to get married as soon as possible. I don't want to take the chance of losing her."

"I see," Caitlin replied flatly. Now she really did understand. It hadn't been her father's idea to have a summer wedding after all. It had been Nicole's. And whatever Nicole's reasons were, Caitlin was sure that love wasn't one of them. She was positive Nicole did not love her father. Somehow, some way, Caitlin knew she was going to have to stop their wedding. But how?

"Caitlin?" Her father was staring at her with an anxious expression.

Seeing his face, she realized there was nothing more she could say just then. He was obviously determined to marry Nicole, and Caitlin knew that if she argued with him any further, it would just drive him away from her. She decided to pretend she was happy for him. She smiled. It was a wan smile, but it was a smile.

"If she makes you happy, Father, then I'm all for you marrying Nicole." Saying that, she rose from her chair. "But now, if you'll excuse me, I really must find Louise. She's waiting for me in the game room. I'll see you later." Before her father had a chance to respond, Caitlin walked quickly to the double doors. Opening one, she slipped through it, with only a quick backward glance at the man who was now staring thoughtfully at the empty fireplace.

The next morning Caitlin's grandmother mentioned the wedding. Mrs. Ryan had asked Caitlin to remain at the breakfast table after Louise had excused herself.

"More tea, Caitlin?"She reached for the silver pot that the maid had just refilled in the kitchen. Dressed for a trip to Ryan Mining headquarters, Regina Ryan was her usual elegant self in a tan Chanel suit and a peach silk blouse. Her silver hair was pulled back in a french twist, and her makeup was both subtle and perfect.

"No, thank you, Grandmother," Caitlin replied with a polite shake of her head. "Louise and I are riding the back hunt course this morning, and I don't want to be too keyed up."

"Of course. I understand completely." Mrs.

Ryan smiled as she went ahead and refilled her own cup. "I won't keep you long, but I'm sure Louise won't mind waiting for a few more minutes. She's a nice girl, by the way. And I understand she is distantly related to the New England Sedgewicks."

"I don't really know."

"Well, I do." Mrs. Ryan's reply was casual, but absolute. "I made it a point to find out about her last fall when you and she first became room-mates at Carleton Hill."

Oh, yes, of course you did, thought Caitlin. She should have realized. "So, what did you want to talk to me about, Grandmother?"

"I'm wondering how you feel about your father's decision to marry Colin's sister," she said. Caitlin noticed the way her grandmother referred to Nicole as an extension of Colin instead of her own person. "I know Gordon discussed his plans with you yesterday after-noon," Mrs. Ryan continued, "and yet you didn't bring up the subject even once at dinner last night, which seemed rather strange to me, considering the importance of the matter."

"But why should I have?" Caitlin replied. "Father and Nicole weren't there."

"But Colin *was* there. He's very happy about the marriage, and he knows how delighted I am. It will bring the Wollmans into the family circle. Quite frankly, I think he was hoping you would express your happiness as well. But, instead, you were sullen and withdrawn. In fact, at one point during the meal you were quite rude to him. He asked you a perfectly civilized question about your summer plans, and you could have at least given him a polite answer."

"I don't remember that, I'm sorry," Caitlin apologized automatically.

"That's no excuse, Caitlin," Mrs. Ryan warned her and then raised the delicate porcelain teacup to her lips and sipped. "One really should be responsible for what one says at all times. Thoughtfulness is the basis of polite society. But, ah, I'm getting off the subject." She put the cup down on its saucer. "I want to know if your sullenness last night had anything to do with the news of your father's engagement. Because if it did, I think it best to nip it in the bud immediately. I'm absolutely thrilled about the union, and I don't want anything, or anyone, spoiling those plans." She looked at Caitlin directly. "Do we understand each other, Caitlin?"

Caitlin looked her grandmother in the eye, defiant at first. But then she realized that, again, she had to go along with everything for the time being. She couldn't raise any more objections to the wedding until she had some kind of proof that Nicole and Colin, too, were up to no good. Purposefully she smoothed her features into a pleasant expression. "Of course, Grandmother.

And I honestly apologize for the way I acted at dinner." She came up with a reasonable excuse. "I must still be tired from the end of school, that's all."

"I understand, dear." Mrs. Ryan smiled. "I'll pass your apology along to Colin."

"Does that mean I may go now?" She started to rise.

"In a moment," Mrs. Ryan said, raising her hand to stop Caitlin. "There is one other thing I wanted to discuss with you. It's about this young man you've been seeing, Julian Stokes. I was wondering when I'm going to have the chance to meet him?"

"Oh. Uh—" Caitlin was thrown off guard. She hadn't expected to talk about Julian. "Well, I'm not really sure. Not right away, though. He's already in Boston, working with Dr. Henry Kramer."

"Hmmm. That's too bad." Mrs. Ryan frowned slightly. "I was hoping to invite him down for a long visit so I could get to know him." She smiled thinly. "However, if that's impossible, what about a weekend?" Mrs. Ryan suggested.

"I—I don't know." Caitlin felt suddenly uneasy as she envisioned Julian sitting there at the table with her and her grandmother. It was difficult to imagine him fitting in. But that thought made her feel like a terrible snob. Quickly she squashed the feeling. Nevertheless,

Caitlin found an excuse. "I really don't think Julian can get any time off. His job demands that he be available anytime—even on weekends."

"How unfortunate," Mrs. Ryan replied. Then she gave Caitlin a penetrating stare. "Tell me, Caitlin, will you two be staying at the same residence hall?"

"Uh, no." Caitlin felt as though someone had just put a hand around her throat and were choking her. Had her grandmother somehow found out that, while she would be officially registered at the dorm, she would actually be spending her time with Julian in the apartment he was house-sitting? But that was impossible. Only she and Julian knew of their plans. She hadn't even told Louise. "The dorms are coed," Caitlin began carefully, "but Julian will be living in an apartment that belongs to a professor. He's going to Europe for the summer, and he wanted someone to live there while he's gone."

"Oh. I'm not sure I approve of coed dorms," Mrs. Ryan said with a frown.

"Oh, don't worry, Grandmother," Caitlin said with a rush of relief. *So that's all that's bothering her.* "There are separate floors for men and women. Don't worry, there'll be plenty of privacy."

"I see." Mrs. Ryan nodded, obviously not completely reassured. Putting down her cup, she rose and reached for her purse at the same time. "I must admit, I still don't approve of your taking this job in Boston. Your father does, however"—she sighed—"so I suppose it's up to me to give in."

"I appreciate it, Grandmother."

Mrs. Ryan looked directly at Caitlin. As she did, a warmth came into her eyes. "I suppose I really would prefer it if you were staying here at Ryan Acres for the summer. I'll miss you." It was one of those rare moments when Mrs. Ryan let her love for Caitlin show.

"And I'm going to miss you too, Grandmother," Caitlin replied honestly.

"Well, perhaps you'll be able to find time to come home for an occasional weekend." Mrs. Ryan smiled. "Now, you and Louise have a pleasant ride, and be careful. Some of those jumps on the back course haven't been attended to since the hunt season last fall."

"Yes, Grandmother."

Caitlin watched as her grandmother left. As she did, the choked feeling returned. This time because of the lies she had told about her living arrangements for the summer. She hated lying.

Caitlin touched the rim of her teacup, idly running a finger around the edge. She had lied for Julian. Was love so wonderful if it turned you into a sneak? Could it be wonderful when it made you feel unhappy about yourself? Something was definitely wrong. She loved Julian, she knew she did. Yet there were moments, such as right then, when her feelings began to waver.

All at once, without meaning to, she thought of Jed. He would never ask her to lie for him. He was too open and honest a person. But, no, it was unfair to compare Jed and Julian. With Jed she had never been in this kind of situation.

With a brisk shake of her head, she drove her thoughts of Jed Michaels out of her mind. What was she doing? That was all in the past. Jed was out of her life. *Julian* was whom she loved now.

Shoving her chair backward, she stood up. She needed a good long ride, a couple of hours to concentrate on nothing but getting Duster safely over one jump and then on to the next. With firm strides she walked over to the sideboard where she picked up her velvet hunt hat and crop. Louise was already down at the stables, waiting.

14

The ride did help, but Caitlin's bad mood returned the next morning and continued for the next several days. It didn't help that nearly every time she saw her father, he was with Nicole. And each time she saw him, he couldn't take his eyes off Nicole long enough to even acknowledge her presence. She might as well have been invisible. More than ever, Caitlin became determined to find some way to stop the marriage from taking place. But at the same time, she felt increasingly helpless about the situation.

She also began having doubts about Julian and their relationship.

Julian called her nearly every day, telling her how much he missed her and how he was looking forward to her being with him in Boston. But his loving remarks didn't have the same effect over the phone that they had in person. She remembered how she had always felt so drawn to him then, as if he exuded some magnetic force. But over the phone, his voice sometimes sounded as if it were that of a very bad actor reciting lines someone else had written. He didn't always sound distant, but it happened often enough that she found herself going over what he had said, looking for reassurance. It didn't help. Instead of absence making the heart grow fonder, as it was supposed to, it was beginning to make Caitlin doubt her feelings.

Caitlin's confusion about her feelings for Julian had not gone unnoticed by her grandmother and father, although they didn't know the reason for her unhappiness.

With plans for the wedding in full swing, Caitlin's father saw her almost every weekend. Although it was somewhat irregular, Nicole and Dr. Westlake planned to be married in the garden at Ryan Acres. Caitlin's grandmother, who had always been especially fond of Nicole, had insisted it be held there. She had then overruled every objection they could come up with, and finally Dr. Westlake had relented, and the matter had been settled. The caterer would erect a large tent on the lawn for the reception, and the same string quartet that had been playing at the party where Dr. Westlake and Nicole first met would be playing for both the wedding and the reception.

It was while Nicole and Dr. Westlake were in

the garden, having just said goodbye to the caterer, that Caitlin's father mentioned his concern about his daughter.

Nicole nodded, realizing that it might be an excellent opportunity to show Gordon Westlake how thoughtful she could be. "I think I have an idea that might cheer Caitlin up a little," she said as they strolled toward the house. Slipping her hand lovingly into the crook of his arm, she told him her plan.

The chance to put the plan to work occurred later that afternoon. Nicole and Dr. Westlake were in the library, discussing their wedding plans, when Caitlin came in looking for a book. It wasn't until after she was already in the room that she realized they were there.

"Oh, I'm sorry," Caitlin apologized. "I didn't know anyone was in here."

"That's all right, honey," Dr. Westlake said, motioning to her to come over to where they were. "We were just going over the wedding plans. I'm afraid I'm hopelessly lost when it comes to this sort of thing."

"Well, I won't disturb you then," Caitlin said noncommittally. She just wanted to escape, and she started backing out of the room.

"Oh, please don't go," Nicole said quickly, stopping her. "I'd really like your opinion." She looked up at Dr. Westlake. "I think we'd both like it if you felt more involved with our wedding plans."

Nicole's plea worked in that it stopped Caitlin from leaving the room. But it was only because Nicole's pronouncement had stunned her. She was certain that Nicole didn't want her involved in the wedding any more than she already was. Caitlin looked at Nicole, trying to figure out what was going on in her devious little mind. She returned Caitlin's stare with a warm smile.

"In fact, Caitlin"—Nicole paused to look lovingly at Dr. Westlake—"we've been talking it over and we would like it very much if you would consider being my maid of honor."

"Your what?" Caitlin said, trying to cover the shock she felt.

"Her maid of honor," Dr. Westlake repeated. "It was Nicole's idea. I didn't say a thing. You know, Caitlin, Nicole could ask any one of her friends. But she hasn't because she wants you—"

"No!" Caitlin broke in, shaking her head. Was her father completely crazy? "No. No, I couldn't." She shook her head again.

"But why not?" Dr. Westlake asked. He was not pleased by Caitlin's impolite outburst.

"Because—because I can't," she finally said. Caitlin searched for a plausible reason why she shouldn't accept Nicole's seemingly thoughtful request. In the end she blamed her job. "I'll be in

Boston, and I'm sure they won't want to give me time off to come back here for the wedding."

"Caitlin, don't be ridiculous," Dr. Westlake said, his scowl deepening. "It's only a summer job. Of course they'll give you time off to come home for your father's wedding. I'll speak to whomever is in charge to make sure they do."

"No, please don't!" Caitlin pleaded.

"Now, Gordon, really," Nicole said, touching Dr. Westlake's arm. "I'm sure Caitlin wouldn't want you running interference for her. She can handle her own problems." She turned to speak to Caitlin. "Perhaps if you just explained the situation, and how much being at the wedding would mean to you, they would understand."

"No!" Caitlin shot back. "I don't want to explain." Nicole's phony facade was suddenly too much for her. "Don't you understand, Nicole? I don't want to be your maid of honor. In fact, I don't want to be at your wedding at all. Period."

"My goodness!" Nicole gasped, her eyes widening with surprise. "I didn't realize you felt that way."

"Caitlin!" Dr. Westlake said, his voice exploding into the charged silence between Nicole and Caitlin. "You apologize to Nicole this instant. And then I want you to explain to me what this incredible rudeness is all about."

Caitlin looked at her father. "I can't apologize because I'm not sorry. And if you don't understand why I'm acting this way, nothing I can say will make any difference."

"You bet I don't understand! And I'm not sure you could say anything that could excuse your thoughtless outburst. Right now, I don't even believe that you're my daughter, that you're the Caitlin I've—" Suddenly he stopped, and a look of understanding came over his face. His voice became low and filled with concern. "Caitlin, would your refusal have anything to do with—with what we discussed when I first told you about the wedding? About the memory of your mother?"

"No, no, that's not it," Caitlin said quickly.

"Well, then what? What is your problem? When I told you I was going to marry Nicole, the only objection you spoke about was that it would somehow tarnish the memory of your mother. But I know there's something else; you have never acted as if you liked Nicole. And you've never given her a chance. All I can see is that you are being rude and thoughtless to the woman I love." He took Nicole's hand. "And with whom I fully intend to spend the rest of my life."

Caitlin looked at the two of them, united against her. She felt as if she were being pushed out of her father's life. Hot, angry tears threatened to spill down her cheeks, but she would not let herself cry. Not in front of Nicole. She would never let herself look weak in front of that woman. Caitlin was certain that the only way to expose Nicole for the fraud she was, was to keep ever vigilant and hope that Nicole make a mistake. That meant keeping the pressure on herself as well. Suddenly Caitlin realized her father was speaking again.

"You know you're hurting me very much, Caitlin. And the only conclusion I can draw is that you won't try to be happy for me. If you did, you would want to be a part of my wedding. Furthermore, you would realize that Nicole wants you to be her maid of honor because she loves me, and she wants to love you, too."

"Oh, Father," Caitlin began, her voice filled with pain, "please don't say any more. Of course I love you. I don't want to hurt you." She paused, looking down at her hands, realizing for the first time how tightly they were clenched. "All right. All right," she agreed. "I'll be Nicole's maid of honor if it'll make you happy." Near tears, she whirled around and ran from the room.

Later that evening Caitlin was in her room getting ready to go downstairs for dinner. She was in her slip and about to step into a long dinner dress when she heard a knock on the door. Thinking it was probably Louise, she called, "Come on in." Caitlin looked up, expecting to see her roommate, but it wasn't Louise. "Nicole!"

"Hello, Caitlin," Nicole said, smiling coolly as she stepped into the room. "I wonder if I might speak to you for just a moment."

"I was just getting ready to go downstairs," Caitlin said in a sharp tone, reaching for a robe and slipping into it.

"I won't take long. I promise," Nicole assured her.

Caitlin sighed. "What is it?"

"Do you mind if I sit down?" Not waiting for an answer, Nicole walked over to a chair near where Caitlin was standing and sat down on the edge of it. Caitlin watched as she smoothed out the silk skirt of her dress to keep it from wrinkling. Nicole looked up at Caitlin but didn't say anything.

"All right, Nicole, what do you want to talk to me about?" Caitlin put one hand on her hip and gave Nicole a direct look.

Nicole smiled calmly. "I want to have a little chat with you about your father. I think it's time the two of us were honest with each other."

"Honest?" Caitlin repeated, her tone surprised.

"Think about it, Caitlin," Nicole went on calmly. "Would I come here where there's no one but the two of us, in order to lie to you?" She shook her head. "I don't think so."

"Get to the point, Nicole." Caitlin folded her arms in front of her. "I still have to finish dressing, and I don't want to be late for dinner."

"Nor do I," Nicole answered, not moving, "but don't worry. When I left, they were just starting cocktails, and what I have to say won't take long."

"I'm listening," Caitlin said impatiently.

"Very well." Nicole's eyes bored into Caitlin's. "I don't want any more scenes like the one in the library this afternoon. I wanted to slap you silly." She paused. "Look, I don't like you any more than you like me, but I will not stand by and watch you trying to turn your father against me. I'm certain that you'd like nothing better than to drive us apart, but it won't work."

For a moment Caitlin could only stare at Nicole in amazement. Her heart was pounding with fury at the woman's audacity. Then she dropped her hands to her sides and collected herself. "How do you think my father would react," she asked in a sure tone, "if I went downstairs and told him what you just said?"

"Go ahead. See how far it gets you," Nicole challenged. "It would be your word against mine. I'll simply deny that I said any such thing. And he'll believe me. He has no reason not to. He knows how hard I've tried to be nice to you, and he knows how difficult you have been in return. So, my dear Caitlin, I'm afraid you've got no choice. Either you continue being difficult, which will only anger your father more, or you do things my way."

"You—you—" Caitlin stared at Nicole for a long, fury-filled moment, then finally managed to spit out between clenched teeth, "you tramp!"

"Ah, I see!" Nicole let out a mirthless laugh. "You can be honest, too. I just wonder who really hates whom the most."

"Does it matter?" Caitlin asked. Her shock had given way to calm, cold anger. She wasn't about to let a scheming little nobody like Nicole get away with ruining her father's life. "You may think you've won, Nicole, but you haven't. And as long as I'm around, you'd better watch your step."

"I'll keep that in mind," Nicole replied evenly. She stood up and walked across the room but turned back just as she reached the door. "Do hurry and finish dressing, dear," she said sweetly. "You don't want to be late for dinner."

15

At the same time that the arrangements for Caitlin's father's wedding were being made, preparations for Emily's engagement party were moving forward. Emily was having a small dinner for her close girlfriends on Friday a couple of weeks before the actual engagement party. Formal invitations had been sent out the week before, but a few days before the party, Emily called Caitlin.

"Oh, Caitlin, I'm so excited. A lot of our old friends will be here. I haven't seen some of them for a year. Morgan's coming. And Gloria Parks and Kim Verdi both said they'd try to make it. Oh, and Diana is coming, too," Emily said.

"Diana!" Caitlin said excitedly. "I can't wait to see her, either." Diana Chasen had gone to Highgate with Caitlin and Emily. The summer after Caitlin's junior year, Diana had nearly died after developing anorexia. But Caitlin had patiently nursed her back to health, and now they shared a special friendship.

"Of course Ginny's coming," Emily went on. "But I guess she's already told you that, knowing how close you are."

"Actually, I haven't talked to Ginny in a while," Caitlin admitted. She didn't explain that she and Ginny weren't talking to each other. Caitlin knew that Emily would want to know what had happened, and she just didn't feel like explaining the whole thing. "It sounds like a lot of fun," Caitlin said in what she hoped was a bright voice. Then another thought crossed her mind. "It is going to be only girls, isn't it?"

"Yes," Emily assured her. "If you're worried about seeing Jed, don't be. He and some of the guys from Highgate that live nearby are having their own get-together that night. He probably won't get back here until long after you've gone home."

Caitlin let out a sigh of relief. "Good. I'm just not sure I'm up to seeing him yet."

"Uh—Caitlin," Emily began hesitantly, "I think you should know that one of the reasons Jed came East for my party was so he'd have a chance to see you. He hasn't exactly said so in so many words, but I know it's true." Emily paused, then went on. "Caitlin, he just wants to talk to you. Can't you at least give him that much time?"

"Emily, I don't want to talk about Jed. He said all he had to say last Christmas."

"Well, the way I heard it, you did most of the talking. Can't you give him one more—"

"No!" Caitlin said emphatically.

"Okay, okay." Emily backed off. "I didn't mean to upset you. I just think it's a shame you aren't together. You should be."

"Well, we're not, so don't go getting any ideas."

"I won't. I'm sorry if I stuck my nose where it doesn't belong," Emily said. Then, in a lighter voice, she added, "So, I'll see you on Friday night, won't I?"

"You couldn't keep me away if you wanted to," Caitlin replied enthusiastically. "And, Emily, I appreciate what you're trying to do. It's just that it still hurts too much. Maybe someday Jed and I will be able to be friends again, but not just yet."

"I understand," Emily said. "I won't say another word about him."

"Thanks." Caitlin hung up the phone. But as she made her way down to the pool to meet Louise, she couldn't stop thinking of Jed.

On Friday, the night of the girls-only dinner party, Caitlin was feeling nervous all over again.

Standing in front of her mirror, she looked at herself. She was wearing a deep blue, drop-waisted dress made of the finest silk. Because the evening was warm, she had swept her hair up and secured it with antique silver combs on either side of her head. She wore the sapphire earrings her father had given her the year before.

But that only reflected how she felt on the outside. On the inside, she felt shaky and unsure of herself. Raising a slim, tanned hand, she held it out, palm-down, in front of her. She was sure that it would be shaking. But as she stared at her hand, it seemed perfectly steady.

"He won't be there. He won't be there," she softly assured her reflection. *But Ginny will be. What'll I say to her?*

Then, with a deep breath, she turned, picked up her beaded evening bag from where it lay on the bed, straightened her shoulders, and went to the bedroom door.

Caitlin and Louise drove to Brookridge Farm in Caitlin's car. Louise had been invited since she was Caitlin's houseguest.

Other cars were already parked along the drive leading to the main house. The Michaelses' estate was a working thoroughbred breeding farm, and the buildings were far less formal than those at Ryan Acres.

As they parked, Louise commented that the house reminded her of some of the farmhouses in Connecticut.

"I've always liked Emily's house," Caitlin said as they walked toward the front door. "I came here a few times last summer when Emily and I were working together at that play school project. And wait until you go inside. It's beautiful, but informal and welcoming, too. Emily's mother has spent years collecting great country antiques."

The door was opened by a maid in uniform. As she stepped aside to allow them to enter, the sounds of laughter and girls chatting greeted them. Then a pretty girl with short brown hair ran toward them.

"Caitlin, hi!" Emily cried happily. Then she put her arms around Caitlin and gave her a hug. Just before she pulled away, she told Caitlin in a low voice, "I'm so glad you did come. I was worried you might change your mind."

"I'm glad I came, too," Caitlin replied in the same low tone.

Then Caitlin turned to introduce Louise. "Emily, I'd like you to meet my friend and roommate, Louise Bates." To Louise, she said, "And this is my very dear friend, Emily Michaels."

Emily smiled at Louise. "I'm delighted to meet you. Caitlin's told me so many nice things about you."

"Thank you," Louise said.

"You look gorgeous, as always," Emily said, turning to Caitlin.

"You look terrific, too," Caitlin told her friend. "And it's not just your dress. You're positively glowing."

"That's love for you," Emily said with a happy smile. "But now, come on in the living room." She put her arm around Caitlin's waist and led the two girls down the hall and into the living room. It was filled with comfortable furniture in soft pinks and peaches, as well as the glowing country wood pieces Caitlin had told Louise about. "I'm afraid everyone's reminiscing about old times at Highgate," she told Louise. "I'll try to switch the conversation to something else."

"Oh, don't do that on my account," Louise assured her. "Caitlin's talked so much about Highgate that I'll probably know just about everything that everyone's talking about."

Soon they were settled on a comfortable couch in the middle of a group of girls that included Morgan, Gloria Parks, and Jane Winthrop. Ginny was nowhere in sight, and Diana had not arrived. Emily explained that she had called to say that she wouldn't be able to come, but that she wanted to be remembered to Caitlin.

There was one maid serving drinks—white wine for those who wanted it, as well as sparkling mineral water and club soda for those who preferred something lighter. Caitlin chose a Perrier, Louise a glass of wine.

Another maid was passing a tray of hors d'oeuvres.

For a while Louise tried to look as though she were really enjoying the conversation that was going on around her. And, for a while, she really did find it interesting. But that was because one girl, Morgan, was dominating the conversation. She had such catty things to say about people that Louise paid attention. But then Caitlin began to talk, and Louise had already heard all of her comments before. Bored, she quietly excused herself, carrying her glass of wine to a pair of french doors that opened onto a patio.

The caterers were busy taking care of the last-minute details required for setting up the dinner on the patio. There were several round tables, covered with floor-length, flowered table-cloths, with centerpieces of mixed summer flowers and candles. Candles in hurricane lamps were elsewhere as well, casting a soft glow over the whole scene.

Idly, Louise walked around, making sure she stayed out of the catering staff's way. Suddenly she noticed someone standing beside the swimming pool, which was directly beyond the patio. The girl was looking down into the water, and the soft glow of the candles floating in the pool reflected up on her face. She looked familiar to Louise, and after a moment she realized it was Ginny Brookes. Louise hadn't seen her since the previous fall when Ginny had come to Carleton Hill to visit Caitlin.

Louise wondered if she should go over and say hello, but Ginny seemed to be deep in thought. As Louise was deciding what to do, Ginny turned back toward the house. Louise watched as she crossed the patio and entered the room, standing just inside the open door. Ginny paused at the doorway and looked toward where Caitlin was sitting.

Ginny! Seeing her former best friend, Caitlin, who had been speaking, was shocked into momentary silence. Unhappiness washed over her as their eyes met. Ginny stared coldly back. Then she broke eye contact and swiveled on her heel to walk purposefully toward another group.

An awkward silence descended on the party. Emily came to the rescue, announcing that dinner was ready to be served.

As the girls filed out to the patio to take their places around the tables, there was some low murmuring. But then that was replaced with more normal chatter as their food was placed in front of them.

The party went smoothly after that.

Eventually, after the final course, raspberry sorbet, was served, Caitlin began to relax as well. It was only later, after several of the guests had already left, that she realized with a shock that it was getting late.

The thought of Jed returning to find her still

there shot through her. Quickly Caitlin rose and said good night to Emily.

"I'm so glad you were here, Caitlin," Emily told her as she walked her and Louise to the front door. "You know that it just wouldn't have been a real party without you."

Emily turned to Louise. "And it was so nice to meet you."

"Thank you for including me tonight," Louise returned politely.

With a last hug for Caitlin, Emily opened the door. Then she paused, her hand on the knob as she heard the sound of a car turning into the far end of the drive.

A flash of fear crossed Emily's face, and she and Caitlin exchanged looks.

"Oh, it's probably only one of the caterers coming for something he forgot," Emily said.

But both she and Caitlin were sure she was wrong.

And a moment later Caitlin's fears were confirmed. Headlights flashed across the lawn, and a Bronco drew to a stop in the drive, just opposite the front door.

The door on the driver's side of the car that Jed always used in Virginia opened, and Jed Michaels stepped out.

16

Jed. Had she really said his name aloud or only thought it? Staring at him standing there looking back at her, Caitlin felt a thousand emotions wash over her. She had known that seeing him again would be difficult, but the moment was a thousand times worse than she'd imagined it would be. She had to fight to maintain her composure. Jed was as handsome as ever.

For Jed it was just as bad. Looking at Caitlin, all he could think of was how beautiful she was. She looked like a princess in her deep blue dress, her dark hair pinned away from her face. He looked down at his own clothes, jeans and a worn-out polo shirt, wishing he were dressed in something more formal, more befitting the beauty he saw before him. It was hardly the way he had planned to look at their first meeting in almost a year. Still he had to speak to her.

"Can I talk to you, Caitlin?" Jed finally asked. Jed spoke softly, but Caitlin heard him clearly.

The sound of his voice broke the trance she had been in since she saw him, and suddenly she remembered all the misery and unhappiness Jed had caused her.

Gathering all of her strength and self-control, she shook her head. "No, Jed. There's nothing for us to talk about." Touching Louise's arm, she said, "Let's go." And without looking in Jed's direction again, she walked down the steps and into the driveway where her car was parked. It wasn't until she tried to insert the key in the ignition that she realized how badly her hands were shaking.

"So, that was Jed," Louise said. *He's gorgeous*, she thought. Louise noticed how nervous Caitlin was. Trying to look appropriately concerned, she added, "Do you want me to drive?"

"No, I'm fine," Caitlin answered decisively. "I'll drive. I'm just fine!" She turned the key, starting the car. Throwing it into gear, Caitlin stepped hard on the gas, spinning the wheels before they took hold. The small sports car roared off down the drive.

Although it had been terribly difficult, seeing Jed again, Caitlin thought as she drove, it had been good for her in one way—it had proven to her that she could face him without crumbling. She knew now that when they met again, she wouldn't lose herself in his deep green eyes or let his crazy, lopsided grin stir feelings of love inside her.

Louise's thoughts were also of Jed. Seeing Jed had been shocking to her, as well, but in a different way. She had decided in an instant that she wanted him. He was more than gorgeous. Jed Michaels was the most attractive boy Louise had ever met. The photograph of him that Caitlin had kept on her dresser all fall term certainly did not do him justice.

Unknown to Caitlin, Louise watched the anger and sadness flicker across her roommate's face in the pale light from the dashboard. As she did so, she tried to figure out a way to make a play for Jed. The problem was, there wasn't all that much time before she had to return to Connecticut. And, if she was going to get to know him, there were a lot more things she needed to know about him, questions she had to ask Caitlin. But not then. Louise knew she had to wait until they had gotten safely back to Ryan Acres, until Caitlin had had time to cool off a bit.

Later, when they were both ready for bed, Louise came into Caitlin's room to say something. Caitlin was sitting cross-legged in the center of one of the lace-canopied twin beds, staring at the blue brocade curtains that had been drawn across the windows on the other side of the room.

"I'm really sorry everything ended the way it did tonight," she told Caitlin sympathetically, sitting down on the other bed. "I mean, you know, with Jed showing up the way he did. It must have been a shock, huh?"

"I guess you could call it that." Caitlin didn't feel like discussing it.

"Caitlin," Louise began, making her voice sound soft and concerned, "do you still love him?"

"No!" Caitlin said emphatically. "Absolutely not! It's just that—" she started to explain. "Forget it. It was just a shock seeing him after all this time, that's all."

"Sure," Louise said, nodding. "I understand."

Caitlin turned toward Louise. "Actually, I'm really glad he did show up. It proved to me that I'm not in love with him anymore."

Louise nodded again. "You know, now that I've seen Jed in person, I do get the impression that he isn't your type. Being from the West and all, I'll bet he's interested in hunting and fishing and all that rugged outdoor stuff, huh?"

"He doesn't like hunting. He hates the idea of killing innocent animals for fun," Caitlin answered without thinking.

"But hiking and rodeos. He likes that stuff, doesn't he?" Louise persisted.

"Well, he did grow up on a cattle ranch, and all that is part of his life."

"What about tennis? Does he like tennis?"

"Yes."

"Does he play well?"

"Yes."

"Does he like pizza?"

"Sure, everyone likes—" Suddenly Caitlin stopped talking. She stared curiously at Louise. "Why are you so interested in Jed all of a sudden?"

"Oh, I don't know." Louise laughed nervously and at the same time shrugged her shoulders. "I guess I was trying to figure out what was so wonderful about him. I mean, you were pretty crazy about him last fall."

"I don't know," Caitlin said in a flat tone. "Look, I don't want to talk about Jed anymore. In fact, I think I'd just like to go to sleep now. I have a bit of a headache from all the noise at the party." She stood up and pulled back the covers on the bed. Then she turned to Louise. "Good night, Louise," she said pointedly.

"Oh, yeah, good night." Surprised at Caitlin's near rudeness, Louise stood up and regarded Caitlin for a moment. Then she quietly walked out the door and into her own room. But she didn't go to sleep immediately. She stared into the darkness, thinking. Caitlin's reaction really had surprised her. For someone who was supposed to be so in love with Julian, Caitlin certainly was upset about seeing Jed. Louise realized that if she was to stand a chance with Jed, she had to make sure that Caitlin didn't waver in her feelings for Julian. She had to do that and reinforce the bad feelings Caitlin already had toward Jed.

It would be tough, Louise knew, because it would mean keeping the two of them apart. And from what she'd seen of Jed, it was obvious that he wanted to talk to Caitlin very badly. He probably wanted to try to get back with her. But Louise wasn't about to let that happen.

Jed was meant to be hers. After all, hadn't it been Caitlin who had given her that fortune cookie with the message that a handsome man would soon come into her life? And Jed certainly fit that description.

17

Louise got up early the next morning, tiptoeing
softly around the room as she dressed. It was
important to be absolutely silent because she
didn't want Caitlin to hear her and interfere with
her plan to win Jed for herself.

Lying awake in bed long after Caitlin had gone
to sleep, she had thought it all out. Her plan was
really quite simple. She just had to keep Jed and
Caitlin apart. She had to make sure that Caitlin
continued to believe that Jed had been dating
Eve—something she and Julian had convinced
her of. And she had to keep Jed from telling
Caitlin the truth.

That was why Louise had gotten up so early.
She was going to call him right then and pretend
to be on his side. And on Caitlin's, too. She
would ooze sympathy, telling him that she knew
the two of them belonged together and that she
was going to act as a go-between to smooth
things over. Instead she would only fuel the fires

of their distrust. She would tell each of them terrible lies about the other. She would make sure that neither of them would ever *want* to get back together. Then, Louise could step in and become Jed's girlfriend.

Two hours later Louise sat alone in a booth in the restaurant at the Twin Oaks Inn, not far from Ryan Acres. She was dressed in a new white sun dress that showed off her long blond hair and deep bronze tan. She knew she looked good as she waited for Jed to arrive.

When she had phoned him, explaining who she was and why she wanted to meet with him, he had jumped at the chance to get together with her. It had been his idea that they meet right then. Louise had gotten permission from Rollins to use one of the staff cars and had taken off for the restaurant.

Louise took a sip of her iced tea, keeping an eye on the entrance to the restaurant. Finally she saw him walk through the door. He was just as fantastically handsome as she had remembered him—tall and trim, his broad shoulders outlined under the blue polo shirt he was wearing. His thick, wavy, light brown hair fell over his brow, making him look boyish and vulnerable. Oh, how she would like to run her fingers through that hair.

She raised a hand to get his attention. When he saw her, he turned and headed toward her table.

"Hello, Jed," she said, giving him her most charming smile. "I'm glad we could get together this soon."

"Listen, I'm really glad you called," he replied, sliding into the seat opposite her.

Louise observed him as the waitress came up and took his order. He looked tired, as if he hadn't slept well.

"Oh, isn't it just terrible?" she said to him as soon as the waitress had left and she had his attention again. "I mean about you and Caitlin. I feel just awful about what happened between the two of you."

"Yeah, well, thanks," Jed said dispiritedly. "The thing is, I came back East because I was so sure that if I could only talk to Caitlin, I could get this mess straightened out. But you saw what happened last night."

The waitress came back with coffee for Jed. Louise waited as he poured some cream into his cup and stirred it. She reminded herself to remember how he liked it.

"Yes, I did," she said in a soft tone. Reaching across the table, she touched the back of Jed's hand briefly, sympathetically. "But I also saw how Caitlin acted. Later, after we'd gotten home, she was so miserable."

"Really?" he asked, looking hopeful. "Because of me? That's a good sign, don't you think?"

"Possibly. That's why I thought I'd call you. I

mean, I can't think of any other reason she was acting that way."

"That's great." Jed seemed to come alive. "Oh, I don't mean I'm glad Caitlin's depressed, but it's great that she might still care for me."

"Well, she didn't actually say so. I mean, not in so many words." Louise tried her best to look thoughtful, knitting her brows in concern. "But I'm pretty sure she does. I just remember how unhappy she was last fall when she started hearing about your dating that girl in Montana. Her name was Eve, wasn't it?"

"Yeah, Eve." He scowled. "But I wasn't dating her. That's the thing," he said, shaking his head. "I still don't understand where she got the idea that I was going out with Eve. It's not like Caitlin to jump to conclusions without any reason. And yet . . ." His voice trailed off, as if the entire matter was still a mystery to him.

"You're really telling the truth? You didn't date this Eve even a couple of times? You know, a movie or a school dance? Enough so that it got back to Caitlin."

"No! Absolutely not. We worked on some class projects together, but that's all!"

"Oh." She smiled at him, showing him that she believed him. Which, of course, she did. "I just wanted to be sure." She hesitated, as if she were thinking about what to do now. "It's just too bad that you didn't straighten this out before Caitlin started dating Julian."

"I wanted to. I really wanted to," Jed said earnestly. "I wanted to fly out here over Christmas, but I couldn't. My dad was very sick, and I had to stay in Montana with him."

"Oh, Jed," Louise said, reaching across the table to touch his hand again, "that's terrible."

"But, look—" Jed began. He pulled his hand away from hers with so little thought that Louise was sure he hadn't even been aware that she'd been touching him. "Why don't I just go over to Ryan Acres right now. I'm just wasting time sitting here."

"No!" Louise said a little too loudly as he started to slide from the booth. "Wait!"

"Why?" he asked, staring at her with surprise. "I've waited long enough as it is." Again he started to leave.

"Jed, listen to me!" She caught his arm. Once he was sitting down again, she went on quickly, "I wanted you to meet me because I know Caitlin won't talk to you now. Look what happened last night. I need to work on her before she'll see you. I need to talk to her, to convince her that you didn't go out with Eve. That whatever she heard, from"—she shrugged—"I don't know where, was wrong. And I need time to convince her that she loves you, not Julian."

"All right." Jed slumped against the back of

149

the booth. A second later he asked, "Do you really think that if you talk to her, she'll see me?"

"I'm positive," Louise stated. "You just have to give me time." She gave him a gentle smile. "Wait a few more days, Jed. What are a few days when you've waited almost a year?"

"I guess so." Jed leaned forward. "But, please, hurry and convince her that she's got to let me see her."

Louise found Caitlin sitting in a chaise on the terrace when she arrived back at Ryan Acres. A book was open on her lap, but she wasn't reading. She was simply staring into the distance.

"Good morning."

"Oh, hi, Louise," Caitlin replied, looking up and giving her a weak smile. "Rollins said you asked to use one of the cars to go into town and do some shopping. Did you get what you wanted?"

What an ironic question, Louise thought. Well, she was working on getting what she wanted, at least. "No. Actually, I just ended up doing some window-shopping," she said as she studied Caitlin's face. "You look a little under the weather. Do you still have that headache from last night?"

"The headache?" Caitlin asked, confused for a

moment. Then she nodded slightly. "Oh, yes, I guess I did have one last night as well," she said, remembering her lie the night before. "And you're right, it's back."

"Then I'll leave you alone. I guess I'll go up and change into some shorts. The day's really turning warm." She started to leave, then turned back. "Oh, by the way," she said in a deliberately casual voice, "I ran into Jed."

"You did?" Caitlin asked. "Where? What did he say?"

"Oh, Caitlin, I'm sorry. I shouldn't have said anything. It'll only upset you," Louise replied, sounding genuinely remorseful.

"Louise, you know I love Julian now. Nothing Jed could say would upset me," Caitlin said in a low, firm voice. "Just tell me what he said."

"Well," Louise began hesitantly, "if you insist. He didn't say anything much until somehow we started talking about Eve. Get this—he said he thought you were selfish to expect him to give up dating while you two were apart. He said he honestly hadn't thought you would mind if he went out with Eve. Isn't that too much?"

"Jed said that?" Caitlin looked stunned. "I don't believe it."

"Believe it," Louise assured her. "I got so mad thinking of you spending all your time writing those long letters to him and not going out on so much as one date. And all the time Jed was seeing Eve. The nerve—"

"Do you think we could stop talking about Jed?" Caitlin snapped, cutting Louise off. "I thought you said you were going up to change."

"Oh, I'm sorry, Caitlin," Louise said sympathetically. "I can't believe how thoughtless I've been. Would you like me to bring you some aspirin, a cold drink? Anything?"

"No, thank you." Caitlin turned her head away. "I just want to be alone for a while."

Louise paused for a moment. Then she walked away.

As soon as she was inside the house, however, she hurried to the library. She had promised Jed she'd phone him with a report as soon as she talked to Caitlin.

When he found out it was Louise on the phone, Jed got straight to the point. "So, will she see me? I'll come right over."

"I'm sorry, Jed," Louise said. "I don't know how to say this, but—I was wrong. Maybe Caitlin's feelings for you aren't as strong as I thought they were. When I mentioned your name, she insisted she wasn't interested in talking about you. What was really bothering her, she said, was being so far from Julian."

"Julian!" Jed almost yelled into the phone. *"Damn him!"*

"Jed, look, I know how you must be feeling."

"No, you don't!" Jed said hotly. Then he calmed down a little. "I'm sorry, Louise. I know you're only trying to help. You're still going to keep trying, aren't you?"

"Well, I don't know," she replied. "I mean, what's the point? She loves Julian."

"I love her!" Jed said heatedly. "Talk to her, Louise. Find a way to get through to her. I'm not leaving Virginia until I talk to her."

"Do you want me to tell her that?"

"If you think it will help, yes."

"I'll do whatever I can," Louise said. "I'll call you in a few days." Louise hung up the phone and smiled.

A few days later Louise was on the phone with Jed again. She was just hanging up as Caitlin walked into the library. Louise started guiltily, the phone still in her hand. She put down the receiver and looked at Caitlin.

"Oh, hi, Caitlin, I didn't hear you come in."

"Who was that on the phone?" Caitlin asked.

"Uh." Louise thought quickly, then it came to her. It was really the perfect opportunity. "It was Jed. I—I didn't want you to know. I wasn't going to tell you."

"What is it?" Caitlin looked concerned. "Has something happened to him?"

"No. Oh, no." Louise put a hand to her chest. "Nothing like that. I'm sorry if I scared you."

"Then what did he want?" Caitlin asked. "Did he want to talk to me?"

"No," Louise replied in a quiet voice. "I'm sorry, Caitlin, but he called to ask me out." She hesitated. "You know, on a date."

"A date!" Caitlin exclaimed. Her face blanched. "Jed wants *you* to go out with him?"

"Well, yes," Louise said, feigning indignation. "Honestly, Caitlin, do you think I'm so horrible looking that he wouldn't want to go out with me? I mean, after all, you're not going out with him anymore. He *is* free, isn't he?"

"Yes, of course he's free," Caitlin said quickly. "And of course you're pretty, Louise. I—I just—" She stopped speaking, unable to go on. She collapsed in a nearby chair. "Oh, I don't know what I mean."

"Oh, Caitlin!" Louise rushed to her side. "I'm sorry for snapping at you like I just did. The reason I didn't want to tell you was because I didn't want to hurt you. I know you don't love Jed anymore. But I also know it's never easy when a friend starts dating your former boyfriend."

"Yes, that's it."Caitlin nodded in agreement, but there was still a blank look in her eyes.

"Then you don't mind if I go out with Jed," Louise ventured.

"No. No, I don't mind," Caitlin said weakly.

"Oh, I'm so glad. I didn't want you to be

154

upset. We're going on a picnic tomorrow. Unless, of course, you want to do something else."

"No. You go on the picnic. Have a good time." She gave Louise a small encouraging smile. "Jed knows the country around here pretty well. I'm sure he'll find a marvelous place for a picnic." She hesitated. There was a lump forming in her throat. "I think I'll spend the day lying by the pool. Maybe I'll write a letter to Julian."

When Jed showed up the next day for what he thought would be a short drive so he and Louise could talk about Caitlin, he was surprised to see her standing on the steps with a picnic basket beside her.

"Hey, do you have other plans?" he asked, leaning his head out of the open window. "We can do this later if you want."

"Oh, this?" Louise said, picking up the basket and moving toward him. "It's just a little snack. I thought we might get hungry driving around in the country. You know, all that fresh air." She smiled. "It's not a real lunch, anyway. Just a little fried chicken, some salad, and fruit. And some cake that Mrs. Crowley made for dinner last night."

She was leaning in through the open window on the driver's side. She tried to make it look as though she were kissing Jed. In reality she just pretended to remove something from his cheek. "A stray eyelash," she explained. The whole thing was for Caitlin's benefit. Louise hoped that Caitlin was hiding behind the curtains in the upstairs hall watching them. Caitlin had said she was going upstairs when they'd passed each other in the front hall a few minutes earlier. Louise knew she wouldn't be able to resist looking out.

"Uh, well, thanks," Jed said. "Here, let me give you a hand with the basket. I'll put it in the back while you get in. I honestly don't think we'll be gone long enough to eat, but since you brought it, well—"

Louise happily handed Jed the basket and ran around to the other side and got in. Jed stowed the lunch in the backseat, and as he turned to climb back in, he glanced up at the windows. But there was no movement. Louise snuggled down into her seat, saying, "Let's go."

You're wrong, Jed, she thought as he put the car in gear, *I'm going to make sure we have plenty of time to eat.*

Louise had been right in thinking that Caitlin might be watching when Jed arrived. Hating herself for doing it, she nevertheless could not help herself. And it was like a punch in the stomach when she saw Louise put her head inside and kiss Jed. That was when she turned away.

Later, lying by the pool, she tried to concentrate on writing a letter to Julian. But after wadding up several sheets of paper with only a sentence or two on each, she gave up. She knew she had no hold on Jed. And until recently she had been absolutely certain she loved Julian. But then why was she feeling so terrible? And why couldn't she get the picture of Louise and Jed sharing a picnic lunch out of her mind?

Louise continued to dance between Jed and Caitlin, spending the next several days telling each of them awful lies about the other. And all the while she tried to make Jed fall for her. Even though he'd never so much as held her hand, Louise had a feeling that if she made the right move, he would melt into her arms. A couple of evenings after their picnic, when Jed was bringing her back from a movie she had suggested they see, she decided the time had come.

The night was perfect for romance. Jed had just shut off the engine and turned in his seat to say good night. The warm, flower-scented air was drifting in through the open windows, and fireflies were winking on and off like tiny stars all around them.

Louise leaned close to Jed, as if to give him a

chaste kiss on the cheek. But, instead, she slid her arms around his neck and gave him a full kiss on the mouth.

Jed was so stunned that he didn't move. Louise pressed her mouth warmly against his, reaching a hand up to twine her fingers in his hair.

Finally Jed pulled away, grabbing Louise's shoulders, and holding her away from him. "Louise, what just happened? What are you doing?"

"Come on, Jed, what do you think I was doing?" she purred. She tried to touch his face, but he blocked her.

"Louise, cut it out!" he said firmly. "Look, I don't know what kind of misunderstanding there's been, but I certainly don't feel about you the way that kiss says you feel about me. I like you, Louise. You're a very pretty and a very nice girl. But to be perfectly honest, about the only way I can think of you is as Caitlin's friend."

"You're joking!" She glared at him. His words were like a slap in the face. In the last few days she had done everything she could to win him over. But when she kissed him, all he could think of was *Caitlin!* She wanted to scream! She could feel the blood rushing to her face and her jaw tightening. She wanted to hit him.

"No, I'm not joking," Jed replied.

She tried to wrench free of his firm grip in

order to strike out at him. He held her tighter, straightening his arms so that she was pushed even farther away.

"Listen to me, Louise. I know that you've been trying to convince me that Caitlin is deeply in love with Julian and that there's no hope that we'll ever be a couple again. But that doesn't stop me from loving her. Do you understand? I still love Caitlin! There's no room in my life for anyone else. *Do you understand?*"

"Oh, yes. Yes, I understand." With a final angry yank, Louise managed to pull herself away from him. "I understand this much, Jed Michaels." Her voice turned vicious. "You are one prize idiot! Maybe I didn't make it plain enough to you, but Caitlin honestly doesn't care this much"—she snapped her fingers in his face—"for you. She doesn't even care if you're alive. She's been sleeping with Julian for months! Months, Jed."

"What?" Jed gasped.

"You've got it!" she spat out. "You heard what I said."

"But—but I don't believe you. She couldn't be." Jed sounded like a person who had just been told that someone he loved had died and he couldn't face the reality of it. "Who told you this?"

"Julian, of course! He brags about it."

"No! No, I don't believe it." Jed wiped his hand across his face. Not his beloved Caitlin.

Louise was still seething. No one rejected her and got away with it. She searched her mind for something that would hurt Jed even more. Then she remembered the letter she had found, the one that had been in that book of Julian's.

"And let me tell you something else. You lost Caitlin to someone who isn't even in her class. Julian—or Jake as they call him at home—is just some poor miner's son. He comes from Rock Ridge, and his daddy worked for Regina Ryan. He's a total nobody." She stopped talking, feeling smug. She waited for him to cringe, to moan, to do something.

Instead Jed just sat absolutely still with a strange look on his face. Finally he spoke. There was a kind of excited quickness to his voice. "Did you say this guy was from Rock Ridge?"

"Yes," Louise answered slowly.

"What's his last name?"

"Stokes," she said, puzzled. "Why?"

"Stokes. Julian Stokes!" Jed was nodding slowly, thoughtfully.

"What's going on? What are you thinking?"

Jed didn't answer. He thought back to that day the previous summer when he and Caitlin had been in Rock Ridge. It had been their last day working on the play school project with the miners' children.

Caitlin had asked him to take a doll of hers to little Kathy Stokes, who had missed the last-day party. But when he had arrived at the Stokeses' cabin, it had been her older brother who had come out to meet him. Then, instead of accepting the doll for Kathy, he had torn it from Jed's hands and smashed the doll's porcelain head into a hundred pieces. He had thrown what was left of the doll into the dirt in front of the cabin.

Julian, or Jake, as he had been called, had lunged at Jed. But the fight had been short. Jed, with a cooler head, had won very quickly. And after Jed turned to walk away, he glanced back to see Julian standing there muttering under his breath. He must want revenge, Jed thought.

Revenge!

Everything was beginning to come together. Somehow, Julian must have planted those rumors about him and Eve. Somehow, Julian had convinced Caitlin that he had betrayed her. But Julian's plot for revenge couldn't have stopped at just getting Caitlin for himself. He had Louise spread horrible rumors about her. Now that he was thinking clearer, Jed was certain that Caitlin couldn't be sleeping with Julian. And he had to warn her about what was going on. But first, first he had to make sure. Suddenly he thought of Matt. Matt Jenks had been on campus with Caitlin all year. He would know. Yes, he'd talk to him.

"Louise," Jed said, turning to Louise, who was still staring at him in confusion. "Thanks for everything. You've helped me more than you'll ever know. But now, I'd prefer it if you'd get out of the car." Jed turned the key, starting the engine with a roar. "But before you do, I'd like to give you a piece of advice. If I were you, I'd leave Ryan Acres just as soon as possible. You're no friend of Caitlin's, and you don't belong here."

Louise quickly opened the door and leaped out—just in time. Without further warning, Jed ground the car into gear and stepped on the gas. He tore off, leaving her standing in the driveway, choking on the exhaust fumes.

18

Saying she was needed at home, Louise left the following day. As Caitlin stood on the stone steps in front of Ryan Acres and watched Rollins drive Louise to Dulles Airport, she realized that she was truly glad Louise had gone. In the past week, as Louise's interest in Jed grew, Caitlin had come to understand what a terribly shallow person her former roommate was. And again her heart wrenched as she thought about how much she missed Ginny. It hurt even more because Caitlin knew it was her own fault that she had lost Ginny's friendship.

She turned to climb slowly up the broad steps. If only she had the chance to do it over again, Caitlin thought, she'd make sure she apologized to Ginny right away.

Well, too bad, she told herself firmly. *You can't do it over again. Life isn't like that. So you'll just have to learn to live with what you've done.*

With a sad shake of her head, she walked

through the house and out to the terrace. The book she had been trying to read all week was there where she'd left it the previous afternoon. She looked at it with an ironic smile. Was that all that was left for her, a novel she wasn't really interested in?

She had lost her grandmother to Colin, her father to Nicole. And now she had even lost Ginny. She wasn't even sure about Julian any longer. Her love for him was like an old photo that was rapidly fading so that now it was terribly blurred in her mind. Jed! Jed was the one whose features she was capable of clearly conjuring up. But he was gone from her life, too.

Just as Caitlin reached down to pick up the novel, one of the maids called to her. "Excuse me, Miss."

Caitlin turned around. "Yes, Margaret," she said dispiritedly. "What is it?"

"I'm sorry to bother you, but there's a phone call for you. It's Miss Brookes."

"Ginny?" Caitlin repeated, her face lighting up. "Oh, thank you, Margaret. I'll take it out here." Caitlin walked quickly to the table where a phone sat. Picking up the receiver, she said in an excited voice, "Ginny, hi! How are you?"

"I'm fine, thank you." Ginny's voice was cold. "I'll be brief, Caitlin. There's something I need to talk to you about."

"Well, great!" Caitlin said, attempting to keep

her enthusiasm up in the face of Ginny's cool tone. "So, okay. Go ahead and talk," she said brightly.

"Not over the phone. It's too important." Ginny paused. "It's about something I feel you have a right to know. Otherwise, I wouldn't be calling." Ginny's last words made it clear that as far as she was concerned, they still were no longer friends.

"Oh?" Caitlin frowned.

"Look, are you free sometime today?" Ginny asked.

"Anytime. Right now."

"Fine. I'll meet you halfway between Washington and Ryan Acres. There's a restaurant, the Broadside Inn."

"I know the place," Caitlin said.

Ginny's voice was crisp. "I can be there in an hour. Okay?"

"I'll be there," Caitlin said and hung up the phone.

Driving to the inn, Caitlin felt nervous about Ginny's news, although she could hardly wait to see Ginny. On the way to the Broadside Caitlin had thought about how wrong she had been to listen to Julian when he had advised her not to contact Ginny and apologize for what had happened in Florida.

She was still sure that Julian had been right when he said that Ginny's crush on him wasn't serious. She also knew that she didn't need to apologize for falling in love with Julian. After all, what was real love compared to a silly crush? But Julian had missed the real issue. Ginny was Caitlin's dearest friend, and she should have called her to set the matter straight as soon as she realized Ginny had left. Well, she was going to apologize right then. Before they discussed whatever it was Ginny had to tell her, she would do whatever it took to win Ginny's friendship back again.

She spotted the tall, lanky figure of her high school roommate as soon as she pulled into the parking lot. Ginny was standing beside the front door, waiting for her to arrive. After quickly parking the car and locking it, she hurried toward the girl. "Ginny! Ginny, hello!"

"Hello, there, Caitlin." Ginny's greeting was as cool as it had been on the phone.

"Oh, Ginny, please don't be this way," Caitlin pleaded. Immediately she launched into the apology she had formed in her mind, ending with, "So, will you please, please forgive me? All I want is for us to be friends again."

At first Ginny drew back. She stared hard at Caitlin. "I think you should have thought about apologizing a long time ago. It's a bit late now," she said with a hard look. But little by little

Ginny's harsh look began to melt. Soon her eyes were shining with tears. Then she was crying. She put her arms around Caitlin's shoulders and hugged her. "I guess I've felt exactly the same way. I mean, I've thought about calling you a million times. I've missed you, too."

"Really?" Caitlin said, crying and hugging Ginny back. "You mean it?" She pulled away to look Ginny in the face. "Honest?"

"Honest!" Ginny answered with a quick nod. "Let's not ever let anything come between us again."

"That's a promise," Caitlin said, smiling.

"A double promise from me."

Ginny paused, and the happy look left her face. "But you still haven't heard what I have to tell you." She shook her head. "After you hear it, I'm not so sure how you're going to feel."

"You mean your news?" Caitlin's face sobered as she nodded. "Well, whatever it is, I guess I'd better hear it. Let's go inside where we can at least be comfortable while you tell me. I mean, maybe I'd better be sitting down."

"Yes," Ginny agreed. "Maybe you'd better be."

Moments later they were seated at a corner table inside the restaurant, sodas in front of them. The waitress had just left.

"Okay," Caitlin said, "you have my full attention. What's going on?"

"All right!" Ginny shook her head, as if to help put her thoughts in order. "Here goes," she said. "And believe me, what I'm going to say is the truth. It's not just a guess." She paused, then said, "I know for a fact that Colin and Nicole are not brother and sister. They are—get this—lovers."

For a long moment Caitlin could only stare at Ginny, speechless. So it really *was* true—what she'd suspected all along. But how? How did Ginny know? "Why don't you start from the beginning and tell me everything you know."

"Last week I had to attend this really formal dinner at the French Embassy in Washington with my parents. I was standing there with my father when a man came over to talk to him—"

"Don't tell me it was Colin?" Caitlin broke in excitedly.

"No, no, nothing like that. The man was an old friend of my father's. Anyway, after a while they started talking about Colin. My father's friend mentioned something about a lawyer they both knew who'd been asked to leave his department to avoid an investigation into his shady dealings. And then he mentioned the man's name. It was Colin. I listened more closely then, because I thought he might be your Colin."

"He's not *my* Colin!" Caitlin put in angrily.

"Yes, but you know what I mean," Ginny

went on. "Anyway, my father's friend mentioned that this Colin had been living in Virginia for the past year and that he was probably involved in another operation just this side of illegal."

"Oh, come on, Ginny," Caitlin argued. "There must be lots of lawyers named Colin in Virginia."

"Just wait a second, Caitlin," Ginny said patiently. "There's more. You see, my dad and his friend continued talking about this Colin, and then my father asked if he was still living with that trashy Nicole. When I heard that, I remembered that you had told me that Colin's sister's name was Nicole. So I spoke up and asked if he'd meant Colin's sister. My father's friend said no, he was certain that Nicole was Colin's *girlfriend*. He said that she's a tall, blond woman, and that she's as sneaky and underhanded as Colin is." Ginny paused for a moment. "It's got to be the same people!"

"Oh, my God, Ginny," Caitlin gasped. "I always knew he was a rat, but I never thought he had actually done things in the past to give him a reputation like this. My poor grandmother! And my father! Ginny, Nicole and my father are going to be married. I've got to do something."

"What?" Ginny asked.

"I'm not sure what, but I'm going to do it right

now!" Shoving her chair back, Caitlin stood up. She picked up her purse, opened it, took out money to pay for her soda. "I'll think about what to say while I'm driving home. Nicole is supposed to be coming over to Ryan Acres this afternoon to meet with the people in charge of the wedding. I just hope she's there."

"Caitlin!" Ginny looked worried.

"Don't worry about me," Caitlin announced firmly. "If anyone needs your concern right now, it's Nicole and Colin."

"From the look on your face, I have a feeling that they're going to need some help." She gave a nervous little laugh. "But seriously, Caitlin, be careful. It's fairly obvious that they're both as crooked as they come."

"I can handle myself." Caitlin's voice was positive. All at once her expression softened. She stepped over to Ginny and bent down to give her friend a last hug. "Oh, Ginny, I really am glad we're friends again." Then she straightened up. "I'll call you later and let you know what happened."

Back in her car, driving toward Ryan Acres, Caitlin felt a rush of exhilaration. She hadn't felt so in control of her life in months. She had acted on her own, without relying on advice from Julian. She was her own person again, ready to face any challenge.

As she drove Caitlin decided what she would

do. Now that she knew that the Wollmans were not who they said they were, she would go straight to Nicole and confront her. Hopefully Colin would be there as well. She would send them both packing, no matter what it took.

Then, after they were gone, she would sit down with her father and grandmother and tell them what she had discovered and what she had done. She knew they would both be devastated, and she wished with all her heart that there was some way she could spare her father and grandmother, the two people she loved most in the world, the pain of learning the truth. But there wasn't, and she was sure that this way they would be hurt less in the long run. She would reassure them both that she loved them very much and hope that somehow the three of them could weather this terrible storm.

Barely slowing her car, Caitlin turned into the estate driveway and sped up the oak-lined lane. At the last minute she brought the car to a screeching halt. With firm resolution, she jumped out and raced breathlessly up the front steps.

19

Caitlin found Nicole in the library. She was sitting at the desk, writing out wedding invitations. A smile touched Caitlin's lips as she thought of how ironic the scene was.

Nicole glanced up when she heard Caitlin enter the room. "Oh, hello, Caitlin," she said. Her voice was flat and cold.

"Hello, Nicole," Caitlin returned the greeting. Then, in a voice that was deceptively pleasant, she said, "I wouldn't bother addressing any more of those envelopes if I were you."

"I beg your pardon?" Nicole said, looking at Caitlin as if she were certain that Caitlin had lost her mind.

"Do you want me to repeat what I just said?" Caitlin asked, her tone still pleasant. "Didn't you understand me? Well, then listen carefully this time." Now her voice hardened. "I suggested you stop what you're doing because there isn't going to be any wedding. Without a wedding, there's no real reason for invitations, is there?"

"Caitlin, dear," Nicole said in a sweet, condescending tone, "I think you've been out in the sun too long. You're not making sense."

"It's funny you should say that," Caitlin replied, "because for the first time in a very long while, everything makes complete sense. Finally, all of my suspicions have been confirmed."

"What *are* you talking about?"

"You and your *brother*, that's what I'm talking about. You see, Nicole, a friend of mine was at a party in Washington with her father recently, and my friend's father happened to bump into an old—uh—business associate of Colin's. An ex-boss of his, to be precise. They were talking about you, too, Nicole." Caitlin stepped closer to the desk, leaning over it so that she could look Nicole directly in the eyes. "Would you like to know what they said about you?"

"Oh, do tell me," Nicole said, almost sneering.

"I believe you were referred to as 'that trashy Nicole.'" Caitlin waited for her words to sink in. "And you know what they said about Colin? They as much as called him a crook. It seems he has quite a reputation as a hustler. But then I guess his *sister* would know that better than anyone."

"That's a lie!" Nicole said, trying to bluff.

"A lie? No, Nicole, I'm afraid not. The way I see it, you and Colin are the liars."

Nicole stared at Caitlin with a hateful expression in her eyes. "No one is going to believe you, you know. Not after all the trouble you've caused this summer."

"Oh, I admit there might be some doubts at first. You and Colin have been very careful to make sure my father and grandmother have believed all your lies. But trust me, Nicole, they will also believe that my friend's father is telling the truth. Maybe you've heard of him, Mr. Ronald Brookes."

Nicole suddenly blanched. The name had obviously struck a chord. Nicole's grand pretenses came tumbling down. In a loud voice she spat out in frustration, "You spoiled little brat!"

At that moment Colin came rushing into the room. Seeing what was happening, he shut the double doors behind him, then strode over to the desk. "What the devil is going on here? I could hear you two all the way down at the other end of the hall. It's a good thing that Regina is out and Rollins is in the kitchen." He looked at Nicole for an explanation, then at Caitlin, and finally back at Nicole again. Neither of them said a word. They just stared at one another.

"Well?" he prompted.

Nicole finally spoke. "She knows, Colin."

"Knows what?"

"She has a friend, Colin. And that friend's father happens to be Ron Brookes. Does that name ring a bell?"

"From Washington?"

"Yes, that's the one."

"Ah," Colin said, turning to look at Caitlin. "Rumors," he said lightly. "Whatever you've heard is nothing but a rumor. That town is filled with them. So what if your grandmother happens to appreciate my services enough to want to give me a present of a few stocks? Is that a crime?" His eyes narrowed as he added, "There's absolutely no proof anywhere that I took them without her permission." He turned to Nicole. "So you see, my darling, there's nothing to get upset about."

"Colin, you idiot!" Nicole shot back. "You just gave everything away."

"Nicole's right," Caitlin agreed. "I didn't even know about the stocks. Now," she said quietly, "may I suggest that you two do the smart thing and leave—right now. I don't want either of you to still be here when my grandmother returns."

"Come off it, Caitlin," Colin said with a grim smile. "First of all your grandmother will believe me, and even if she doesn't, do you really think that Regina Ryan would admit she had been taken? I suspect not. So you see, little girl, you've really got nothing on either Nicole or me—nothing that anyone will take seriously anyway. You can say we're not brother and sister, and we'll simply disagree. Don't you think your grandmother and father will believe us?"

He paused to glance at Nicole. "I think we'll stay right here. And when Regina returns, we can all have a pleasant lunch on the terrace while she bores us talking about what's going on at Ryan Mining. And you, Caitlin dear, can bore us with stories of your morning tennis game or your ride on the back course or whatever you did to wile away the morning hours."

Caitlin ignored Colin's nasty little speech. Keeping her voice calm, she repeated, "I really do think you two should take my advice and leave. I don't want to call the police and have them hurt my father and grandmother with the kind of questions they would find it necessary to ask, but I will if I have to."

Nicole's confidence was renewed by what Colin had said, and now she turned again to Caitlin. "Perhaps the real reason you don't want to call the police is that, as Colin said, you have no proof that we've done anything wrong. As for what your friend's father said, Colin is also correct in saying that Washington is full of jealous people who would like nothing better than to discredit anyone as successful as—my brother."

"Yes, do keep your story straight, Nicole," Caitlin replied smoothly. "You're going to need all the help you can get. You see, it really doesn't matter if I can prove anything. Do you think my father would still want to marry you with that kind of doubt cast on your reputation? And, Colin, do you think my grandmother would continue to trust you with Ryan Mining's legal business after she'd heard from a trusted friend like Mr. Brookes that you have a reputation as an embezzler and a hustler? I don't think so." Caitlin smiled triumphantly. "You know, it's funny," she added. "You two don't even look like distant cousins. Now, I would definitely suggest you take me up on my offer and leave without a scene."

"If you like to play games, Caitlin dear," Colin replied, seeming in perfect control, "I will be happy to play, too. But you'll lose. I know you're bluffing about calling the police or anyone else, so don't try to scare us away."

"I've never been good at those kind of games," Caitlin said, sighing reluctantly. "So I guess I'll just have to go ahead and do what I said I'd do." She reached for the phone on the desk. "Because you'll soon find out I meant every word I said—"

"No! Stop!" Nicole yelled out. She put her hand over Caitlin's, keeping her from dialing.

177

"Never mind. I believe you." She looked at Colin. "Colin, you may think you're good at bluffing, but I don't want to find out if you're not. I have no desire to tangle with the police or Ron Brookes."

"Nicole, pull yourself together!" Colin insisted. "It's Caitlin's word against ours, and she's been having problems with her father ever since he told her about your engagement. He'll just think this is one more attempt to make trouble."

"Well, Nicole?" Caitlin asked, her voice cool and threatening.

Nicole hesitated, looking first at Caitlin's hand, which was tanned and strong beneath her own. Then she looked up at Colin and finally back at Caitlin.

"Nicole?" Caitlin persisted.

"Oh, all right, Caitlin," Nicole said, relenting. "You win. There's no need for the police, at least not as far as I'm concerned." She shot another look at Colin. "If you want to call them about *him*, do it after I've gone."

Nicole left, pausing briefly at the door to turn back and ask, "Colin, are you coming or not?"

"Well, *Colin*?" Caitlin echoed Nicole's question.

As Nicole had done, Colin hesitated. But, with his partner deserting him, he obviously felt less sure of himself. Finally, without looking at Caitlin, he walked out the door.

Caitlin's heart was pounding. She stood in the library, listening. Finally she heard the click of Nicole's high heels in the front hallway, then the front door being opened, and finally the subsequent slam. A few minutes later the sound of Colin's Mercedes 450SL driving away echoed in her ears.

It was over, just like that. Caitlin wanted to throw her head back and laugh, but suddenly she realized that she was shaking terribly. Her knees felt as though they were about to give out.

She managed to make her way to the chair by the desk. Closing her eyes, she sat down and took a deep breath to calm herself. She had won! It had all happened so fast, too. A year of suspicions and fear had come to an end in minutes. And best of all, she felt confident for the first time in months. The confidence she'd lost by depending on Julian had returned.

Suddenly Caitlin thought of Jed. She had to see him. She knew now that she had run away from him that night at Emily's party because she had been afraid of what he might say, and she had been afraid of her own feelings. She had known even then that she still loved him, and she had run away because of those feelings. Perhaps she just hadn't been able to bear the thought that Jed might not feel the same. Perhaps if she hadn't let herself be smothered by

Julian's love, she would have had the courage to find out sooner. But now she had the courage. Whatever Jed felt, good or bad, she had to finally find out the truth. She picked up the phone again and dialed the number at Brookridge Farm.

20

"Oh, hi, Caitlin," Emily said when she answered the phone.

"Hi, Emily, is Jed there?" Caitlin asked, her voice almost impatient.

"No, I'm sorry, he's not. He left a little while ago."

"Do you know when he'll be back?"

"Not really. He just said he had some things he had to take care of as soon as possible. He seemed kind of preoccupied."

"Oh," Caitlin said in a disappointed voice. A moment later she said, "Listen, Emily, can you leave him a message for me?"

"Sure. Of course."

"Could you tell him that I need to talk to him. It's very important."

"I'll make sure to tell him," Emily answered. Then she hesitated for a moment. "Caitlin," Emily continued in a hesitant voice, "maybe this is none of my business, but does this mean that maybe you two are going to get back together?"

"I honestly don't know, Emily," Caitlin admitted. "I just want to talk to him."

"Well, I'll keep my fingers crossed. And I just know that once you two start talking, you'll realize that you're crazy not to be together."

"Don't get your hopes too high, Emily," Caitlin warned. "A lot has happened since Christmas."

"I know," Emily said. "But I can't help hoping. I love you both, and nothing would make me happier than to see you together again. You are going to be at Ryan Acres, aren't you? So Jed can call you as soon as he gets back?"

"Yes, I guess so. Sure, I'll wait right here."

"Well, I know he'll call you just as soon as he gets home." Emily paused for a moment, debating in her mind whether to mention her news to Caitlin. She finally decided that Caitlin should know. "You know, I was going to call you today anyway. I heard some terrible news this morning."

"Emily, what is it?" Caitlin asked, her voice filled with concern.

"It's about Kathy Stokes," Emily said.

"Kathy *Stokes?*" The name caught Caitlin off guard, reminding her of Julian. But then she remembered that the little girl who had been one of her favorites at the play school in Rock Ridge the previous summer had been named Stokes as well. "Is she sick, Emily? Has there been some kind of accident?"

"No, nothing like that. It's her father. Remember how sick he was with black lung disease?"

"Yes," Caitlin replied impatiently.

"Well, he died. Early this morning."

"Oh, no," Caitlin gasped. "Poor Kathy. She must be terribly upset. And poor Mrs. Stokes." Caitlin paused as she thought for a moment. "Listen, Emily, I'm going to drive out there and see if I can help in any way."

"What about Jed?"

"Tell him—tell him that I'll be back in a few hours. And please tell him not to go anywhere until we've had a chance to talk."

"You bet I will," Emily promised. "And don't worry. I don't think he's going to move so much as a foot from the phone until he can talk to you. Oh, and, Caitlin," Emily added, "tell Mrs. Stokes how sorry I am. And Kathy, too. Tell them I'll drive over tomorrow to see them."

"I will," Caitlin replied. She hung up the phone and went to get her purse and car keys. Then she looked around for Rollins to let him know where she was going so he could tell her grandmother. She found him in the kitchen. On the table nearby was a large number of freshly cut flowers. Barnes had just brought them in so that Catherine, one of the maids, could arrange them in vases for the house. Caitlin told Rollins where she was going, and then wrapped some flowers in a wet paper towel with aluminum foil over it. She was taking them with her to give to Mrs. Stokes.

About ten minutes after Caitlin had left Ryan Acres, Jed came roaring up the driveway. Rollins answered his thunderous knock on the front door. They spoke to one another briefly and then Jed raced back down the steps to the Bronco. Rollins shook his head doutbfully as Jed tore back down the drive. When he got out to the road, he turned in the same direction as Caitlin had.

Caitlin drove her car into the small town of Rock Ridge. She then turned down the narrow, rutted road that led to the Stokeses' cabin.

Mrs. Stokes answered the door when Caitlin knocked. Her little girl, Kathy, was hanging on to her skirt, her eyes red from crying. "Yes?"

"Hello, Mrs. Stokes. I'm Caitlin Ryan, from Project Acorn. I knew Kathy last summer."

"Of course. Won't you please come in, Miss Ryan."

"Thank you." Entering the room, Caitlin handed Mrs. Stokes the flowers she'd brought. "I just came to say how sorry I was to hear of your husband's passing." She looked down at Kathy. "Hi, honey. Do you remember me?"

Kathy didn't respond, but continued to hang on to her mother's skirt.

"She's upset," Mrs. Stokes said, apologizing.

"Of course," Caitlin said, bending down to Kathy's level. "I know it's been a long time since you saw me. Do you remember the fun we had at the center last summer? I remember you."

"'Course I remember you," Kathy said in a small voice.

"I'll go put these in water," Mrs. Stokes said. Looking at Kathy, she added, "I'll be right back. Will you keep Miss Ryan company?"

"Listen," Caitlin said, standing back up. "Why don't I do that? And maybe fix you a cup of tea while I'm at it." She reached for the flowers she had just given Mrs. Stokes. "Why don't you sit on the couch with Kathy. I'm sure I can find my way around the kitchen."

"Oh, thank you, Miss Ryan." Mrs. Stokes sighed, obviously relieved that someone was taking control for the moment. "I'd just about reached the point where I wasn't sure what to do next."

"Well, a cup of tea is a good place to start," Caitlin said sympathetically.

Caitlin put water on to boil. Then she arranged the flowers in a juice bottle, and brought them into the living room. She made the tea and put two mugs and a glass of milk for Kathy on a tin tray, as well as thick slices of homemade bread and some butter. But as she put down the tray, she noticed that Kathy had fallen asleep. Her head was resting in her mother's lap.

"You look as though you could use some sleep yourself," Caitlin said in a low voice as she handed Mrs. Stokes her tea. "Maybe after you've had some of that, you might try to take a nap. I'd be happy to keep an eye on Kathy."

"Oh, that would be so nice. I'd be so grateful. If you don't mind, that is."

"Of course not. I'd be happy to do whatever I can to help. That's why I came."

"Bless you."

Spying a pillow on a nearby chair, Caitlin went over and picked it up. "Here, let me put this under Kathy's head. You'll both be more comfortable that way," Caitlin suggested. Gently, she began lifting the little girl's head when suddenly the front door came crashing open, then slammed back with a bang.

Caitlin's first reaction was to protect Kathy from whomever it might be. She looked down at the little girl and saw that she was awake and struggling to sit up. Then Caitlin turned and, along with Mrs. Stokes, looked toward the door. Julian!

What on earth is he doing here? Caitlin wondered. *He's supposed to be in Boston.* For a moment she could only stare at him in confused amazement. Then she heard Kathy cry out.

186

"Jake! Jake! You came home. Mama said you wouldn't, but I knew you would. I knew it!" Kathy scrambled up off the couch and ran toward Julian.

But Julian just stood there, stunned, as his little sister tried to hug him. He was staring at Caitlin sitting in the shabby living room where he had grown up. He wanted to turn and leave. He wanted to somehow erase the last few moments from her memory—so that she would never know he lived there. But her stare was just as searing as his, and Julian knew that Caitlin would never forget what she had just seen.

Caitlin watched as Kathy looked up at Julian expectantly. But Julian didn't pick her up as the little girl had thought he would. It was as though he hadn't even noticed she was there. It was at that moment that Caitlin understood everything. No wonder Julian had never wanted to tell her about his background. No wonder he was so ambitious. Her mind reeled, and she groped for something to say. She had a million questions, and they all crowded into her mind at once.

"Jake. Jake," Kathy cried, breaking the silence.

Finally Julian realized that his sister was trying to get his attention. He started to reach down to touch her shoulder when the door burst open again.

"Jed!" Caitlin cried in shock and astonishment. She couldn't believe how angry he looked.

He didn't look at her, but at Julian. His eyes were narrowed with fury. "I thought I'd find you here. When I went to Ryan Acres a while ago to warn Caitlin about what you really are, Rollins told me that this was where she was headed." Jed had moved closer to Julian while he was talking, and now he grabbed him by the collar of his shirt. Their faces were only inches apart. "I think we need to talk, Julian," he spat out. "Outside!"

"Jed, stop!" Caitlin screamed, rushing forward and trying to throw herself between the two men. "Stop it, please!"

But they were both so angry that they totally ignored her. Jed dragged Julian outside.

"Stay here, Kathy," Caitlin told the little girl. Then, with what she hoped was a reassuring smile at Mrs. Stokes, she rushed outside as well.

Jed had pushed Julian against the outer wall of the cabin, and he was accusing him of all the terrible things he now knew Julian had done. "Admit it, Stokes," Jed demanded in a harsh voice, "you're the one who made sure that Caitlin and I broke up last Christmas, aren't you? Aren't you?" Jed's face was red with fury. "Louise told me some things last night, and I figured it out from there. Then I went to talk to my friend Matt Jenks to make sure my suspicions were correct. You started those rumors to make Caitlin think I was seeing Eve. You and Louise," Jed said, pulling at Julian's shirt with such force that he was almost choking him. "Isn't that right? Answer me! And say it loud enough so that Caitlin can hear it!"

"Y-you're choking me."

Jed suddenly realized what he was doing and loosened his grip on Julian's shirt. "All right. Now tell her, you creep. Tell her the truth, tell her how you were only using her, or I really will choke it out of you."

Looking past Jed's shoulder and seeing the horror on Caitlin's face, Julian realized just how much his position had changed. There was only one hope left for him. He grabbed it. He began telling her the truth, but in a way that he hoped would elicit her sympathy.

"Yes, yes. All right," Julian said slowly. "Let me go and I'll tell her everything."

Jed let go of Julian's collar, but he didn't move away.

Julian reached up and rubbed his neck, then ran a hand nervously through his thick, dark hair. "Caitlin, look—I admit that I did do those things that Jed accused me of. It was for revenge at first. Oh, Caitlin, you've got to understand what it was like growing up in a place like this. I'm so much better than this rotten town, I've always known it." He looked at Caitlin. "Remember that Christmas when you came to Rock Ridge with your grandmother? You were handing out presents and there was a little boy who tried to touch your coat, and you—"

"Oh, my God!" Caitlin gasped. "That was you?"

"Yes, it was me." Julian shook his head as he remembered the bitter shock of that moment. "So, don't you see, Caitlin? How could I not want to hurt you, to hurt the Ryans. You were— are—everything I have never been.

"And then last summer," Julian continued, "it was as if it was happening all over again. You came here to do your good deeds, *to help the poor*. You even sent Jed up here with that doll, that *used* doll, for Kathy."

"But I loved that doll," Caitlin protested. "Bitsy was my favorite. That's the only reason I wanted Kathy to have her."

"And do you know what he did with it?" Jed asked. In answer to his own question, he continued, "He smashed it into the porch railing. Kathy saw it all."

"No!" Caitlin cried, putting her hand over her mouth.

"Oh, Caitlin, Caitlin," Julian pleaded, "can you ever forgive me? I'm so very sorry—about everything that's happened."

But Caitlin was shocked beyond words. Throughout Julian's confession, she had stood rooted to one spot, watching as Julian's magnificent qualities turned to dust in front of her. His need for revenge and his passionate hatred made Caitlin weak and sick inside.

Jed's reaction was entirely different. His fury exploded from him as he lunged at Julian, grabbing his shoulders. "How could you?" he shouted. "How could you treat her so callously? You are the lowest—"

"Jed, stop!" Caitlin finally cried. Her voice was strangled with pain. "Leave him alone."

"No!" Jed replied, turning his head to look at Caitlin. "He hurt you, and I won't let him get away with it. I want to—to destroy him the way he tried to destroy you."

Caitlin shook her head sadly. "I think he's already done that to himself." She had been speaking to Jed, but she was looking straight at Julian. Then, turning to face Jed, she added, "Kathy and Mrs. Stokes need him now. Let him go."

"What do you mean? Why do they need him?" Jed asked.

"Julian's father died this morning, Jed. That's why I came here. I came to see if I could be of any help." Her gaze flickered briefly toward Julian. "I suppose that's the reason Julian is here, too."

"Oh, God!" Jed immediately released his hold on Julian, but he shot a warning glance at the

191

other man. "I'm only doing this for them, not you. Don't forget that."

Julian quickly took advantage of his freedom and stepped toward Caitlin. "Caitlin! Don't leave me!" he cried.

Jed moved quickly, however, blocking him. And then, with another quick step, he moved to Caitlin's side and put his arm protectively around her. "Come on. Let's get out of here."

"No, Caitlin, don't go. Stay!" Julian pleaded. "I need you. I love you! Please, you must believe me." He reached toward her, begging her. "Even while I was trying to get revenge, I realized how much I loved you."

Julian's words, however, did not weaken Caitlin's resolve. Her voice was strong and firm as she faced him and spoke. "Well, you've had your revenge, Julian. Now you're free, and I'm free as well. I've paid my price for being a Ryan, and I'm finished with the guilt you made me feel." She raised her chin slightly. "And I'm finished with you."

"But—but, Caitlin, I love you. Please!"

Julian's pleas fell on deaf ears. With Jed's arm protectively around her, Caitlin turned away from Julian and toward the cabin. Recognizing that he had lost, Julian stormed down the driveway and disappeared around the bend.

Jed had looked questioningly at Caitlin when she turned in the direction of the cabin. Seeing the question in his eyes, Caitlin said softly, "I can't leave without saying something to Mrs. Stokes. And Kathy, too," she said. Jed gave her a worried look. "It's okay. I don't think Julian will come back just yet. He loves his mother and sister too much to risk another scene. I'm sure of that."

"All right," Jed agreed reluctantly. "But, please, Caitlin, don't be too long. I'll wait out here just in case Julian does come back."

"Thank you, Jed. But I honestly think everything will be okay," Caitlin replied. With that, she entered the cabin.

Mrs. Stokes was seated on a straight-backed chair near the door, and Kathy was huddled, frightened, against her mother's skirt. Her head was buried in Mrs. Stokes's lap. Tears ran down Mrs. Stokes's face, and she looked up at Caitlin with an expression that was a mixture of shame and grief. As Caitlin approached her, she looked as though she were about to say something, but she just ended up shaking her head numbly.

Filled with compassion for the older woman, Caitlin quickly knelt down beside her. She put her hand over Mrs. Stokes's hand and squeezed it gently. "It's all right. Everything's going to be all right," she assured the woman in a low, calming voice. "The fight is over, and no one was hurt." She patted Mrs. Stokes's hand. "It was an old misunderstanding, and it's all taken care of now."

"Oh, Miss Ryan," Mrs. Stokes began. "I just don't know what to say about all of this. I—" She broke off, a tired sob replacing her words. But Caitlin noticed that Mrs. Stokes's hand had relaxed a little, and Caitlin was glad the older woman was calming down.

"You don't have to say anything," Caitlin continued softly. "I'm sure Julian will be back just as soon as I leave, and he'll help with everything. He loves you." She stroked Kathy's back. "And he loves Kathy, too. Very much. I can tell." Caitlin stood up, but then she bent down long enough to kiss Mrs. Stokes's cheek. "If you need anything, *please* call me."

"Th-thank you," Mrs. Stokes replied. Then somewhat hesitantly, she added with a wan smile, "I will. I promise."

Feeling that she had done all she could for the moment, Caitlin left the cabin and went back outside to where Jed was waiting. He held out his hand to her as she came down the steps. There was a look of concern on his face. "Are they okay?"

"Not yet," Caitlin replied as she took his hand. Then she added with a sad smile, "But I think they will be. Mrs. Stokes is a strong woman, and she'll get through this just fine. I know she'll help Kathy be strong as well."

"Good." Jed squeezed Caitlin's hand. "But I think we really should go home now. You're too upset to drive. We'll take my car and come pick yours up tomorrow."

"Yes," Caitlin agreed, giving Jed the smallest of nods. "Yes, Jed, please take me home."

In silence they walked over to the Bronco, which Jed had parked nearby. Tenderly Jed helped Caitlin into the front seat, then went around to the driver's side and got in. He started up the car and drove away. But as soon as they had left the mining community behind, he stopped again. Pulling the Bronco under the shade of a tree, he switched off the engine and turned in his seat to face Caitlin.

"Do you know how very much I love you?" he said, reaching up and gently brushing her cheek with his hand.

"I think I do," she answered softly, feeling herself tremble as she looked into the intense green of his eyes and realized just how long it had been since she had done that. His eyes were so honest, so filled with love. How could she have doubted him?

"I'm really glad," Jed said with a small laugh. "Because for a long time I wasn't sure you'd ever say anything like that to me again." He took a deep breath. "Oh, Caitlin, I'm so sorry for everything that has gone wrong between us. I was such a jerk about listening to those rumors about Julian. I guess I never really believed them, but still—" He stopped and shook his head. Then he continued, "Hearing them just made me so crazy."

"Oh, Jed, it was just as much my fault," Caitlin protested. She put her hands lightly on Jed's shoulders. "I never should have believed the things I heard about you and Eve. It was stupid of me, and I should have known better. I should have had more faith in you."

"And I should have been more understanding. I should have reassured you more often about how much I love you. I guess I just didn't realize how hard it would be to be apart." Jed pulled Caitlin gently into his arms. His voice turned husky as he said, "But just so long as I can reassure you now, and tomorrow, and the day after. I love you, Caitlin, I love you."

Then he stopped talking as, pulling her even closer, his lips met hers. It was a long, slow kiss—long enough to try to make up for all of the kisses they had missed during the past year.

Francine Pascal

In addition to collaborating on the Broadway musical *George M!* and the nonfiction book *The Strange Case of Patty Hearst*, Francine Pascal has written an adult novel, *Save Johanna!*, and four young adult novels, *Hangin' Out with Cici*, *My First Love and Other Disasters*, *The Hand-Me-Down Kid*, and *Love and Betrayal & Hold the Mayo!* She is also the creator of the Sweet Valley High series. Ms. Pascal has three daughters, Jamie, Susan, and Laurie, and lives in New York City.

Diana Gregory

Growing up in Hollywood, Diana Gregory wanted to become an actress. She became an associate TV producer instead. Now a full-time writer, she has written, in addition to other books, three young adult novels, *I'm Boo! That's Who!*, *There's a Caterpillar in My Lemonade*, and *The Fog Burns Off by Eleven O'clock*, plus several Sweet Dreams novels. Besides writing, her other love is traveling. She has lived in several states, including Virginia, where she stayed on a horse farm for a year. She now calls Seattle home.

Caitlin

We hope you enjoyed reading this book. All the titles currently available in the Caitlin series are listed at the front of the book. They are all available at your local bookshop or newsagent, though should you find any difficulty in obtaining the books you would like, you can order direct from the publisher, at the address below. Also, if you would like to know more about the series, or would simply like to tell us what you think of the series, write to:

Kim Prior
Caitlin
Transworld Publishers Ltd.
61–63 Uxbridge Road
Ealing
London W5 5SA

To order books, please list the title(s) you would like, and send together with a cheque or postal order made payable to TRANS-WORLD PUBLISHERS LTD. Please allow the cost of the book(s) plus postage and packing charges as follows:

All orders up to a total of £5.00: 50p
All orders in excess of £5.00: Free

Please note that payment must be made in pounds sterling; other currencies are unacceptable.

(The above applies to readers in the UK and Republic of Ireland only)

If you live in Australia or New Zealand and would like more information about the series, please write to:

Sally Porter
Caitlin
Transworld Publishers (Aust)
Pty Ltd.
15-23 Helles Avenue
Moorebank
N.S.W. 2170
AUSTRALIA

Kiri Martin
Caitlin
c/o Corgi and Bantam Books
New Zealand
Cnr. Moselle and Waipareira
Avenues
Henderson
Auckland
NEW ZEALAND

IT ALL STARTED WITH THE

SWEET VALLEY TWINS

For two years teenagers across the nation have been reading about Jessica and Elizabeth Wakefield and their High School friends in SWEET VALLEY HIGH books. Now in books created especially for you, author Francine Pascal introduces you to Jessica and Elizabeth when they were 12, facing the same problems with their parents and friends that you do.

DON'T MISS ANY OF THE BOOKS IN THIS EXCITING SERIES:

No. 1   BEST FRIENDS

No. 2   TEACHER'S PET

No. 3   THE HAUNTED HOUSE

No. 4   CHOOSING SIDES

No. 5   SNEAKING OUT

No. 6   THE NEW GIRL

No. 7   THREE'S A CROWD

COMING SOON:

No. 8   FIRST PLACE

No. 9   AGAINST THE RULES

TRUE LOVE!   CRUSHES!   BREAKUPS!   MAKEUPS!

Find out what it's like to be a COUPLE

Ask your bookseller for any titles you have missed:

1 CHANGE OF HEARTS
2 FIRE AND ICE
3 ALONE, TOGETHER
4 MADE FOR EACH OTHER
5 MOVING TOO FAST
6 CRAZY LOVE
7 SWORN ENEMIES
8 MAKING PROMISES
9 BROKEN HEARTS
10 SECRETS
11 MORE THAN FRIENDS
12 BAD LOVE
13 CHANGING PARTNERS
14 PICTURE PERFECT
15 COMING ON STRONG
16 SWEET HEARTS
17 DANCE WITH ME

Coming soon . . .

COUPLES SPECIAL EDITION
SUMMER HEAT!

18 KISS AND RUN